These Are Not the Words

These Are Not the Words

Amanda West Lewis

Groundwood Books
House of Anansi Press
Toronto / Berkeley

Published in 2022 by Groundwood Books / House of Anansi Press
groundwoodbooks.com

Groundwood Books respectfully acknowledges that the land on which we operate is the Traditional Territory of many Nations, including the Anishinabeg, the Wendat and the Haudenosaunee. It is also the Treaty Lands of the Mississaugas of the Credit.

We gratefully acknowledge for their financial support of our publishing program the Canada Council for the Arts, the Ontario Arts Council and the Government of Canada.

 Canada Council for the Arts   Conseil des Arts du Canada

 ONTARIO ARTS COUNCIL
CONSEIL DES ARTS DE L'ONTARIO
an Ontario government agency
un organisme du gouvernement de l'Ontario

With the participation of the Government of Canada
Avec la participation du gouvernement du Canada | Canadä

Poems on pages 25, 76, 93 and 121 were written by Gary Allen Lewis sometime in the 1960s. Excerpts on pages vii, 35, 76, 108, 160, 161, 162, 171–72, 182, 204 and 205 from *The Tempest* by William Shakespeare, *The Riverside Shakespeare*, Houghton Mifflin Company, 1974; 82 and 118–19 from *The Tale of Genji* by Lady Murasaki, translated by Arthur Waley, Houghton Mifflin Company, 1935; 56 and 57 from *A Coney Island of the Mind* by Lawrence Ferlinghetti, New Directions, 1958; 73 from "Snow-White and the Seven Dwarfs," *Grimms' Fairy Tales* by the Brothers Grimm, translated by Mrs. E.V. Lucas, Lucy Crane and Marian Edwardes, Grosset & Dunlap, undated; 11 and 12 from "Tell Me More" by Billie Holiday, 1940, copyright 1978 by Edward B. Marks Music Company; 103 from "Side by Side" by Harry Woods, 1927; 73 from "Miss Brown to You" by Richard A. Whiting and Ralph Rainger, with lyrics by Leo Robin, 1935.

Library and Archives Canada Cataloguing in Publication
Title: These are not the words / Amanda West Lewis.
Names: Lewis, Amanda West, author.
Identifiers: Canadiana (print) 2021023539X | Canadiana (ebook) 20210235470 | ISBN 9781773067926 (hardcover) | ISBN 9781773067933 (EPUB)
Classification: LCC PS8623.E96448 T54 2022 | DDC jC813/.6—dc23

Design by Michael Solomon
Taxi photo by Tim Hüfner, Unsplash. All other photos courtesy of the author.
Printed and bound in Canada

Groundwood Books is a Global Certified Accessible™ (GCA by Benetech) publisher. An ebook version of this book that meets stringent accessibility standards is available to students and readers with print disabilities.

Groundwood Books is committed to protecting our natural environment. This book is made of material from well-managed FSC®-certified forests, recycled materials and other controlled sources.

MIX
Paper from
responsible sources
FSC
www.fsc.org   FSC® C016245

For my mother
who taught me to choose

Were you thinking that those were the words,
those upright lines? those curves, angles, dots?
No, those are not the words, the substantial
words are in the ground and sea,
They are in the air, they are in you.

Walt Whitman, "A Song of the Rolling Earth,"
Leaves of Grass

I have done nothing, but in care of thee
(Of thee my dear one, thee my daughter)

William Shakespeare, *The Tempest*

One

525 East 14th Street
New York
January, 1963

Strangers in the Night

The living room is a foreign country at night.

I'm in my nightgown, at the edge of the dark. My feet are bare, still warm from bed.

Pops is at his desk. His office lamp, the one with the green shade, makes a small pool of light. He's staring at a contact sheet of photos. His brass cube magnifier is in his right hand, gliding over the pictures. A drum brush in his left hand swish-slaps on the edge of the table. Ollie the cat is draped over his shoulders.

Deep quiet, except for a voice from the record player.

Tell me more, and more, and then some…

Deep dark, except for flickering light from the TV, a movie with no sound.

Deep corners, past the light. Slivers of movements. Murmurs. Strangers.

Sweet smoke curls around a candle flame.

I am a ghost crossing this midnight territory, the foreign country between the world of my bedroom and the familiar shore of the kitchen.

"Hey, Miss Missy."

Ira hovers like a dancer in the doorframe, balancing on the balls of his boxer feet. His gold tooth gleams in his dark face like sunshine.

Pops says Ira is my guardian angel. Mom says Ira keeps an eye on things. Ira says we're his family.

I reach for a glass, fill it with water from the tap. "Thirsty. Can't sleep."

Ira opens the fridge and gets a bottle of milk. He pours some into a pot and turns on the stove. He reaches to get my favorite mug out of the cupboard, the one with the chocolate-brown horse head on the side.

"Your momma's at her night class. There's a few folks over for the music."

Ira answers questions I haven't asked.

He spoons sugar into the milk and stirs it slowly.

Sweet steam rises in the mug as he pours. His delicate fingers curl around the face of the horse. For a moment our hands hold the cup together — brown and strong, white and small, the warmth shared between us.

Slow sounds drift from the living room into the kitchen.

"...pass it...the coast next week...I'll bring it tomorrow..." *But I never will hear enough.*

Words I can't put together. "Does Mom know there are people here?"

"Ira's here. Nothing for you to worry 'bout. Now you take that milk and skibble on back to bed. Ain't nothin' as good as sittin' in bed sippin' on a cup a milk."

The steam coats my face.

"Your momma will be back soon. We just need to be keepin' things quiet. Don't want Captain Daddy Pops to be gettin' upset."

I glide like a silent ice skater through the living room, balancing the warm cup like a prize. The TV light flickers. Dots of burning cigarettes flare and fade in the dark corners. Smoke drenches the room like a fog.

Pops does not look up. The strangers do not look up. I skate the cup back home to my bedroom.

Family Is

Family is me and Mom and Pops, and Ira when he's around.

Mom has a mother who lives across the ocean. Mom has a father. *"I don't want anything to do with him."*

Pops has a father who lives in California. Pops has a mother. *"I don't want anything to do with her."*

Family is me and Mom and Pops, and Ira, if he's around,

In the 14th Street Loop
Of Stuyvesant Town
On the island of Manhattan
In the middle of New York
On the edge of North America
In the Northern Hemisphere of the Earth
Third planet from the Sun
Solar System
Milky Way Galaxy
Universe.

Family is me and Mom and Pops, and Ira when he's around.

"Mostly safe, and mostly sound," says Pops.

My Real Name Is
Miranda Billie Taylor

My last name is Taylor, the same as Pops. And Mom. That's how you know we're family.

Miranda is a girl in Mom and Pops's favorite play, *The Tempest*. She was the only daughter of a great magician. Prospero.

Prospero loved Miranda and wanted to protect her from all of the evils of the world. So they lived on a deserted island and Miranda grew up strong and beautiful and smart. But one day Ferdinand, the king's son, shipwrecked on the island and he and Miranda fell in love.

It was a happy ending for Miranda. But Prospero had to give up all his magic powers. It was the only way he could leave the island.

Billie was a famous jazz singer. Billie Holiday. The greatest jazz singer of all time. A beautiful woman

Who started as a waitress in Harlem

Who taught herself how to sing

Who sang about heaven and blessing the child

Who sang about strange fruit and flames

Who sang about getting by and no regrets

Who sang to make sense of the world.

Billie's story didn't have a happy ending. She died when I was eight years old. Pops told me, "Billie Holiday couldn't live without her smack." I don't know what that means, but I know she left behind her story and her music. I listen to her songs all the time.

I'm Miranda Billie Taylor.

But everyone calls me Missy because of Corky.

Corky and Me

I live in 5D, #525 East 14ᵗʰ Street. And my phone number is Oregon 3-9198.

Corky lives downstairs in 4D, #525 East 14ᵗʰ Street. And her phone number is Oregon 3-2653.

Corky's real name is Courtney, but when I was three, I couldn't make my mouth go around the sounds and her name came out as Corky.

My real name is Miranda, but when she was three, Corky couldn't make her mouth go around the sounds and my name came out as Missy.

We go to a school called Friends Seminary. We call it Best Friends Seminary.

When we were in first grade, we learned that the Meeting Room was for being quiet and listening, even if no one was talking. Especially if no one was talking. Because that is what you do at Best Friends Seminary. We learned how to lie down quietly on the pews in the Meeting Room during rest period. But when no one was watching, Corky and I stretched up our hands and made puppet signs to each other.

When we were in second grade, we played horses at recess. We cantered in the schoolyard, pawing the ground and neighing until our throats hurt.

When we were in third grade, Corky's parents got divorced. Sometimes, on weekends, Corky and her little sister Patty stayed with their father, David, in a high-rise beside Central Park. He let me stay with them once. We went for a picnic in Central Park and ate potato chips and drank Fresca, even though we weren't allowed pop in Stuyvesant Town. David bought paper-doll books for us to share. Shirley Temple. Barbie. Lucy and Desi and little Ricky. Corky and I helped Patty cut out clothes.

When we were in fourth grade, Corky and I joined Reading Club. We read *The Borrowers* and made little books and little matchbox beds for little people. We read *A Cricket in Times Square* and heard him singing in the newsstand at the corner of 14th Street and Avenue B.

When we were in fifth grade, we read all the Nancy Drew books and acted out scenes. Corky was Nancy because she loves solving mysteries just like Nancy Drew. Also, she's a really good actress, so I let her be the star. I played Nancy's best friend George because she's really smart and she doesn't get scared easily. We let Patty be Bess, because Bess is small and a bit of a scaredy-cat.

Now we are in sixth grade. We love our teacher Mrs. Nault who says her name the French
way, so it sounds like "Know." Corky says, "Mrs.
Nault *knows* everything!" We've joined the
French Club and we wear berets, and when we
meet in the lobby we say, "Bonjour, mon amie."
At the end of the day we say, "Adieu, mon amie."

Mrs. Nault is teaching us to sing "La Vie en
Rose." Corky sings "mon coeur" with her hand
over her heart. I sing "la vie" with my hand
stretched out to Corky.

Stan and Ollie, and Sailboat

We have two Siamese cats, Stan and Ollie, named after Pops's favorite comedians, Stan Laurel and Oliver Hardy. Sometimes, late at night, Laurel and Hardy come on the television and Pops wakes me up so I can watch Sad Stan and Angry Ollie.

"This is another nice mess you've gotten me into," says Ollie.

"My father played golf with Ollie," says Pops. And he shows me a picture of men with golf clubs. Pants buckled at their knees. Socks in crisscross patterns up their legs. Ollie is smiling, not angry. Pops points to a face I've never seen. "That's your grandfather Hal."

Last fall, Stan had a kitten. It turned out Stan was a girl cat, and Ollie was a boy cat. Pops called the kitten Sailboat because he said he'd always wanted a sailboat.

But Sailboat died when Pops rolled over in bed. Sailboat should have been sleeping with Stan. But Pops had always wanted a sailboat.

Mom and I buried Sailboat under a tree outside the apartment. I collected dandelion flowers for Sailboat's grave and sang one of

Pops's favorite songs — "Summertime" — even though my voice isn't at all like Billie Holiday's so it sounded all wrong. But Pops wasn't there, so maybe it didn't matter.

We didn't see Pops for a few days after Sailboat died.

Double Life World

Most mornings, Pops wears a gray suit, carries a briefcase and his Hasselblad camera to go to work in the office of Pepsi-Cola Corp. He's editor-in-chief of the magazine, *Pepsi-Cola World*.

Some mornings, Pops works at home, spreads contact sheets of photographs on the table. He marks them in red with a sticky grease pencil, chooses the image and writes up the stories for *Pepsi-Cola World*.

Most nights, Pops wears a black sweater and carries his drumsticks out the door to clubs in basements where jazz lives in Harlem. In Harlem, no one knows *Pepsi-Cola World*.

Some nights, Pops doesn't come home. He swallows some pills to keep him awake and stays at the clubs till the dark turns to dawn, stays at the clubs till Ira brings him home, stays in the music.

Mom calls it Double Life World.

My Twelfth Birthday

Grilled Cheese Sandwiches.
   Triple Chocolate Cake.
   Vanilla Ice Cream.
   Mom and Corky and Patty.
   And Ira.
   Corky gives me a book of French poetry, with translations in English so I can understand what they say, and a record of Edith Piaf singing "La Vie en Rose."

   Patty gives me a plastic horse the color of wood, with my name engraved on the horse's rump. *Missy.*

   Mom gives me a new sketch pad and a set of fifty-two different watercolors with names like alizarin crimson and Payne's gray, raw sienna, viridian green and ultramarine violet. Colors she's learning about in her art class.

   Ira gives me an old turquoise ring. It's banged up and there's a big dent beside the stone. But it's a beautiful color and Ira says the stone is ancient, "full of special powers for our Miss Missy." It's too big, but he gives me a chain so I can wear it as a necklace until I grow into it.

   Everyone sings Happy Birthday to You and

I blow out twelve candles and everyone claps.

Everyone except for Pops, because he isn't there.

Pops Leaves Me a Poem

I find it beside my bed in the morning with a white stone shaped like a heart on top.

> *The sky loves to hear you*
> *Sing on a hill*
> *The grass is thrilled*
> *Just to be near you.*
> *And now that you're born*
> *The earth can stand still.*
> *The spring is your morning.*
> *The world is your teething ring-o.*

I know it's a special poem he wrote just for me. It's the best birthday present ever. I put it and the white stone shaped like a heart into the heart-shaped treasure box he and Mom gave me for Christmas.

It's the first thing I've put in the box. It's that special.

My Twelfth Birthday: Take Two

"Happy Birthday, Princess."

I'm asleep when Pops turns on the lamp beside my bed, the one he gave me when I was ten, the one made with a stirrup and a tiny palomino colt.

I'm confused because my birthday was yesterday.

My eyes don't want to open. But I make them behave.

Pops has a finger to his lips.

"Shhh. Your mother's sleeping."

The clock says 11:30.

"I'm taking my princess to the ball."

Pops is wearing one of his big warm smiles. "I'm taking you to the Hickory House to see Marian McPartland. I've got us a table down front. Just us. A special birthday present, because my princess is twelve. Now you be quick." His smile looks a bit wobbly and maybe a bit too big for his face. His blue eyes — cerulean blue, Mom calls them — are shining. "Your coach is waiting."

On the street outside there's a horse and carriage and a man in a top hat. Soft fat snowflakes drift down, dotting the horse's back. He twitches a black ear and tosses his head. The bridle jingles.

The driver holds my hand as I climb into the carriage. I have on my favorite party dress, velvet blue with satin trim, and my shiny black patent shoes. Pops tucks a blanket around my bare legs. Mom would tell me to wear tights. But even I know you don't wear woolen tights to see a singer in a jazz club.

I'm glad I brought my tiny white fox fur stole. My California grandmother sent it to me at Christmas, even though I've never met her, and I named him Furdy. I wore him for our New Year's party on the rooftop, but I've never worn him out late at night to go to a jazz club. He's clipped around my shoulders with his yellow glass eyes facing out, as if he's looking forward to an adventure.

The horse's hooves begin a gentle clip-clop on the nighttime streets. As we leave the curve of Stuyvesant Town and head along Fourteenth, he picks up speed, trotting past yellow taxis waiting to pick up rides.

We turn up Park Avenue and the top of the Empire State Building is shimmering like a Fourth of July sparkler in the midnight sky. The carriage weaves through the traffic. We jingle past Times Square and people point and wave, and so I wave back.

Pops is humming. His drumsticks ding-ding-da-ding, ding-ding-da-ding on the back of the driver's seat. I can feel him riffing off the horse's steps and the jingle of the bridle. We're a traveling jam session.

We turn and slow down on a street filled with neon signs. 3 Deuces. Club Carousel. Jimmy Ryan's. There are people everywhere, spilling off the sidewalks, taking over the streets from the cars. Traffic has slowed to the pace of walking. There's a jumble of piano and drums and laughter.

The driver stops outside a dark building. Pops holds my hand as I step down from the seat. "My princess." The driver bows low and I curtsy. The horse nods his head up and down. I feel like I'm the star of my own movie.

We walk down the steps and Pops pushes open the heavy iron door. Inside, a man in a tuxedo leads us around a circular bar with a fringed awning. He takes us to a booth with soft leather seats that squeak as I slide in, scooting my bottom over to make room for Pops. The man in the tuxedo whisks away the Reserved sign from our table.

The Hickory House is filled with laughter and smoke, the clacking of ice cubes and the buzz of talk. On the walls there are huge paintings of men playing football, and hundreds of photographs signed by famous people.

In front of us is a small stage with a piano, drum kit and stand-up bass. There are women sitting at the bar in long mink coats and little square mink hats. I pull Furdy tight around my shoulders and try to sit like Mom when she's all dressed up. Stylish, Pops calls her.

A waiter in a white suit and black bowtie places a drink in a wide tall-stemmed glass in front of me. There's a red cherry sitting on top of mound of pink crushed ice. A pink paper umbrella pokes out of the top.

Pops has a plain brown drink with ice cubes. "Happy Birthday, Princess. Cheers!"

My drink is sticky sweet. I can only take small sips before the back of my throat feels glued together. I nibble on the cherry.

People come over to our table to say hello.

"Missy, this is Barry. Missy, this is Elaine. Missy, this is Zev."

They all smile and say, "Happy Birthday, Missy!" and clink their glass to mine.

"Going to get another drink." Pops goes to the bar and visits more friends. I eat the salty peanuts from the bowl on the table.

Curls of smoke make patterns in the lights.

My eyes start to sting so I close them.

Loud applause. I snap my eyes open. A lady in a shiny dress the color of a peach glides onto the stage and sits at the piano. I see her long feet hovering above the pedals. Ready. She nods to the man playing the drums beside her. He lays down a beat and the room settles in.

Pops slides back into the booth beside me, and I snuggle into him. Marian McPartland starts to play, and the piano notes bounce in between the drums and the bass. Her dress is low at the back, and I can see her muscles making the music. It looks like she's squeezing the tune out of the piano. Her fingers run up and down the keys, like the keys are too hot to stay on. But then the notes stretch out and get soft. Her fingers are stroking the keys like they're pillows. The tune gets quiet. It nestles into my ear like a secret.

The drum brushes swish like whispers. The bass takes the tune, and it bumps against my skin. I close my eyes and see ice-white snowflakes swirling. I can smell Pops's aftershave, so I know he is close by. The snowflakes drift...

"Wake up!" Pops is pushing me. "Marian is playing Happy Birthday for you!"

Everyone in the club is standing, singing and

looking at me. A piece of cake, frilled with layers of frost-white icing like a ballerina tutu, is sitting in front of me. A candle sticks out of the top. Everyone claps.

"Now make a wish," says Pops.

I'm confused from sleep. Our table is littered with empty glasses.

"Make a wish." His eyes look steel gray, not cerulean blue. I hear the slight edge of a growl as his warm, sticky breath washes my face.

I take a deep breath.

I wish I knew what to wish for. I'm worried I'll get it wrong.

Words That Last a Thousand Years

I don't tell Mom about the Hickory House. Pops said it was our secret. A special night. Because I'm twelve.

At school, Mrs. Nault's chalk dances across the board. It's as though the words are springing out of chalk dust.

> *Strange. Your lute music,*
> *These matchless flowers,*
> *And all beauty of the night*
> *Has tempted no other feet*
> *To linger outside your door.*

"That poem was written in Japanese over a thousand years ago by Lady Murasaki Shikibu. She wrote the very first novel, a book called *The Tale of Genji*."

Words. One thousand years old. Magic on the blackboard.

"This is what *The Tale of Genji* looks like."

Mrs. Nault holds an art book open. On one side is a painting of a Japanese lady sitting at a desk and looking out to sea. On the other, Japanese letters twirl down the page.

"The poem is called a tanka. It starts off as a haiku, with five syllables, then seven syllables, then five syllables. A tanka adds two more lines, each with seven syllables. Thirty-one syllables in all. Tankas were sometimes written by two people as a kind of game. One person writes the first three lines, the haiku, and another writes the last two, the response. Writing a tanka with a friend is a way of having a very special conversation."

Corky and I write a tanka:

> *When we grow up, we'll*
> *be famous writers and we'll*
> *travel to Japan*   *(Missy)*
> *where we will drink tea and gaze*
> *at the ocean together*   *(Corky)*

I write a tanka for Pops, to thank him for the Hickory House.

TANKA FOR MY BIRTHDAY
by Miranda Billie Taylor

> *Her shoes are soft peach.*
> *Her foot stretches. She presses*
> *down on the pedal.*

Notes elongate. Sad music
fills the room. Spring will be late.

When I get home, I put it under his brass cube magnifier. That way I know he'll see it the next time he looks at his contact sheet photos for *Pepsi-Cola World*.

Remember the Rules

When Corky sleeps over we always make a place for her to sleep on the floor, even though we know we'll wind up sharing my bed. Stan is spread out beside me. Ollie is in the living room with Pops. Mom is at her painting class. Ira is with his new girlfriend.

Pops is working. We need to be quiet. We need to stay out of his way.

Corky grabs my copy of *The Tempest*. The book falls open to our favorite scene. She kneels at my feet.

"Cornelius Van Dyke the Third." Corky grins.

Cornelius is the most stuck-up boy in our class, but she knows I have a crush on him. He'd be a perfect Ferdinand. She bats her eyelashes.

"The very instant I saw you, did
My heart fly to your service, and there resides,
To make me a slave to it, and for your sake,
Am I this patient log-man."

Corky grabs both of my feet between her hands, as though she is praying.

I try to say my line—*"Do you love me?"*—but I can't stop laughing. I'm laughing so hard I start hiccuping. I'm laughing so hard I think I might pee! We're both laughing so hard that—

WHAM!

The door smashes open, banging against the wall.

"WHAT THE HELL IS GOING ON!"

Pops. Gray, tight, huge. Corky and I are frozen. A black-and-white photo where no one breathes.

"I'M TRYING TO WORK AND YOU'RE SCREECHING! WHAT THE HELL'S SO GODDAMNED FUNNY?"

I forgot rule number one. Don't make Pops angry.

There's a warning hiss.

Stan.

In two steps Pops has Stan hanging by the scruff of her neck—

Pops screaming, "Shut up you stupid cat!"

Stan snarling and spitting—

"Don't hurt her!"

—sounds lost as he hurls her down the hall like a bowling ball—

Snap. Blackness.

"Go to sleep." The door slams.

Frozen silence.

The Earth spins around the Sun, the Sun orbits through the Milky Way. Leaving us behind.

When do I start to breathe again?

When do I hear a small scratch at the door?

When do my muscles move?

When do I reach for the doorknob, the door-knob that crashed into my wall?

I open the door an atom-sized crack, and Stan streaks in. My hand turns the knob back in place with a quiet click.

In the dim light, I see Corky curled in her floor bed, blankets to her chin. Stan is crouching, tense. I reach out to pick Stan up, but she turns away, stretches her paws to Corky and begins to knead her covers. Pull, release, pull, release. A tiny purr escapes. Stan parades in a tight circle and curls up on the floor, leaning into Corky.

I step over them and into my bed. I slide my toes under my sheets. There's still a warm spot from where Stan was.

"I'm sorry," Corky's voice is small, muffled by her pillow. Lonely miles away.

Corky's "Sorry" makes it real.

The room is a garbled time signature. Sunny, dancing 4/4 shattered into stuttering 7/8.

I put *The Tempest* under my pillow. I hear Stan purr, but there is empty space at the foot of my bed.

Purring claims the darkness.
Remember the rules.

Another Tanka

I leave it on his desk, with a blue barrette on top.

31 SYLLABLES
by Miranda Billie Taylor

We made too much noise
When you were working. I'm so
Sorry I forgot.
Don't worry, Stan is fine now.
Please don't still be mad at me.

Drawing Infinity

On Monday, Mrs. Nault shows us how to draw linear perspective. "Parallel lines appear to converge at a vanishing point in the distance."

A vanishing point in the distance.

I hold my wooden ruler tight.

I draw one line. It is just a line until I draw another.

A long V.

I look at Corky. But her back is to me and her V is hidden.

I trace over my V. Make it darker, stronger. Two lines that come together. Converge.

I draw horizontal lines inside the V. They get shorter and shorter the farther back they go until they vanish.

"Objects in the background appear to diminish in size as they recede," says Mrs. Nault.

I draw trees on either side getting smaller and smaller the farther back they go.

A magic train track to infinity.

I look at Corky's back. I can't see her train track.

I shut my eyes.

I hear the clatter of the infinity train.

It sounds like a drum solo.
A drum solo of a vanishing train.

There Is So Much to Learn

After school, the door is unlocked. I open it to a silent picture.

Pops at his table, holding his magnifier cube over contact sheets. Mom on the couch, a copy of *Art Magazine* in her hand. Ollie draped over Pops's shoulders. Stan on Mom's lap.

I step into the picture, and it comes to life.

Mom's smile sparkles onto her face like the tinkling bells of an ice cream cart on the first day of spring. "I've got some news."

Pops is very still. His cigarette isn't lit. His glass is empty.

"Tony—that's my professor—asked me to apply to do my master's. He says my work shows promise."

I balance my schoolbooks on the edge of the coffee table. "What's a master's?"

"It's like a new grade level. It's a huge privilege. It's hard work, but once you have one, you can teach. Tony asked me to be his teaching assistant next year."

Ollie's tail swishes across Pops's shoulders. Pops doesn't move.

"*Another* year of school?" I try not to sound

disappointed. Mom spends a lot of time at school.

Stan tumbles off as Mom puts her magazine on the table and gets up to hold my shoulders. Her smile is working at being contagious. "I'm still finding out what I don't know. There's a lot to learn."

"Mrs. Nault taught us perspective today." I wonder if Mrs. Nault is a better art teacher than Tony.

"There is a lot more to art than perspective! Besides, my paintings are abstract, so I don't even use perspective."

"What do you mean, they're abstract?"

I've never seen Mom's art. She said she's afraid to show us until she gets better.

"They aren't paintings of things. They're colors. They're feelings."

Swish-slap. Swish-slap. We both turn to look at Pops. His drum brushes are in his hands. Swish-slap. Swish-slap. Like he's waiting to lead in the bass, ready to bring in the riff. Ollie's blue eyes stare at us from Pops's shoulders.

I look at Mom.

Suddenly, Pops explodes out of his chair as though it has kicked him. Ollie bounces down the middle of his back to the floor.

"Let's get some Chinese food to celebrate!" He claps his hands like a magician, and I half expect food to appear out of thin air. "Come on. Let's go to China Boy."

China Boy! It's my favorite restaurant. We go there every Christmas and eat with chopsticks and our fingers, and we always get fortune cookies and our fortunes almost always come true. Pops grabs Mom and whirls and dips her in his arms, like they're in a ballroom.

"Moo goo gai pan to celebrate my sugar!"

She's laughing and I'm laughing and I'm thinking about sweet and sour spareribs as Pops sets her upright.

"First a picture. Family Portrait time."

Family Portrait. We do one for every special occasion, like Christmases and birthdays, or when Pops got a promotion at work, and when Mom got accepted to art school. Sit on the same couch in the same positions every time. Doing Family Portrait today says that Mom doing her master's is special.

I realize we haven't done one for my birthday this year.

Pops's swirling movements are double-time.

"Yup. Family Portrait. Family Portrait of your mother leaving us."

The swirls stop. The room is ice. Pops is whisking his camera onto a tripod, setting up the timer.

Mom's hand reaches forward but stops. It hangs in the space between them.

"We've been through this, Paul. I'm not leaving. I'm just staying in school for another year. It isn't going to change anything."

Pops whirls around. He imitates Mom but makes her voice like caramel toffee. "Tony asked me to be his teaching assistant." His face is twisted. "Yes, Missy, your mom's a lot smarter than both of us, so she's gonna become a professor and leave us so she can paint pictures."

"Paul, that's not true!"

"I may not have some fancy degree in art, but I make pictures, too, and get paid good money for them."

Ollie is crouched across the room staring. Stan has disappeared. Pops's voice is a growl. The camera is in its Family Portrait position, facing the couch.

"SIT!" he barks. "I'm starting the timer."

"Paul, please—"

"You have ten seconds. Do not be late." His eyes are volcanoes.

I was late once. I'm just a blur in that picture.

"Never be late," Pops had said. "You see? You look like a ghost. You have to be there in time. We all have to be there."

"Ten, nine, eight—"

Mom isn't moving. We all have to be there.

"Five, four—"

I snap into my place in the center of the couch, Mom plunks in on one side, Pops on the other.

"SMILE, GODDAMN IT!"

Click.

And in one smooth movement, Pops gathers his camera from the tripod, grabs his jacket and disappears behind a slammed front door.

Silence settles on Mom and me, on the couch, on the empty tripod, on the room, like dust. Ollie's tail jerks as he stares at the closed door.

Slowly, Mom reaches over and takes my hand in her lap. She starts to pet it like it's a kitten.

My hand tenses and I'm going to pull it away but Stan jumps up and curls over the lump of our hands.

"I would never, ever leave you, Missy. You have to know that."

Mom is still stroking my wrist, but softer, with her thumb. Under Stan's soft belly.

I put my free hand on Stan's back. A Stan sandwich, with purring up and down.

Rule number one. Never make Pops mad.

"Would you like to come to the studio on Saturday? To see my paintings? I'd like to show you. We could go to the Automat afterwards."

The China Boy fades. Fortune cookies fade.

Perspective. A vanishing point in the distance. Things in the distance get smaller.

I feel my head nod slowly.

Crashing Waves

There's a frosty slip under the sunshine when Mom and I head to the Lexington Avenue bus. Mom's art school is in Washington Square. I'm nervous about what I'll say when I see her paintings. I don't think I know the right words. But I can't wait to go to the Automat for lunch.

I thought the studio would have bright white walls and a big open space, like a gallery. But it's a mess! There's a clutter of easels, stools and benches, an avalanche of papers sliding off a desk, an overflowing garbage can, grimy heaps of paint-splashed rags. It smells stale with cigarette smoke and old nail-polish remover. The dark wood floors are gouged and thick with splatters of paint.

This is what she loves?

"This is it. Where the magic happens." Mom spreads her arms wide, as though she owns the whole room. "My pieces are in my locker. I'll get them out and set them up so you can see them properly. Close your eyes and don't open until I say so."

I close my eyes and listen to her walk. It's a different rhythm. — 3/4 time, like a waltz. A different Mom. I hear the slide of canvases onto easels.

I hear her take a deep breath.

"Okay. Open your eyes. Wait! Open them slowly. Don't say anything. Just look."

The room is throbbing! Swirls of color, canvas after canvas, colors of tropical birds, of sunsets, of raspberries with orange sherbet. Colors like Billie singing "Laughing at Life." Paintings like the happiest days in spring. The colors mix and blend and snap off into the room.

"How do you do that?"

Mom's laugh is Indian yellow. "Each color has a different wavelength, a different energy. It's all about what happens when the waves crash together."

Crashing waves.

"I didn't know you could do that!"

Mom's smile is an ice-cream sundae.

But then I see one painting that backs into itself instead of flying around the room. January dusk, grit, dirty sidewalk grime, dead leaves in the gutter. Billie Holiday singing "Strange Fruit."

"Is that one yours?"

Mom looks at the painting like it's someone she doesn't want to recognize.

"Sometimes the crashing wavelengths cancel

each other out. It's called graying out."

All I can see are steel swirls. A tidal wave that can't find the shore. An ocean where the rules don't make sense.

"Sometimes the colors know you better than you know yourself."

I don't want to know what Tony thinks about that painting. Those are not the colors of Mom.

The Story of Me

The Automat is shiny and gleaming and fresh. Rows of glass doors with shiny brass knobs, each a little glass showcase, open up to different things to eat. Small plates of sandwiches, cakes, little dinner rolls, meatloaf. Little doors. A world of choices. Mom says I can have anything I want.

"It's hard to choose."

I reach up and turn a shiny brass knob. Lemon chiffon cake.

Mom puts my cake on the tray and heads to the coffee urns.

I wish there was an Automat at Friends Seminary. Corky and I could choose a different lunch every day. No more cafeteria surprise.

"Why didn't you go to art school when you were young?"

She presses the lever, fills a cup, pours in cream from a glass pitcher, making her coffee the color of her camel hair coat.

"I was at school when I met your father."

She sounds like she's starting a fat book. We sit at a table on the side, against the wall. I spread out the linen napkin on my lap.

Pops says Mom is elegant. I practice looking

elegant as I pick up the heavy silver fork and break off a piece of cake.

"I was at Hunter College, in my last year. I loved school. In fact, I was in love with my professor."

I almost choke! "What?! You were in love with someone who wasn't Pops?"

Mom smiles her lopsided smile, the special one for me. "Well, I thought I was in love. Herb and I were going to get married as soon as I graduated."

"Herb?! You were going to marry someone named Herb?"

"He was so kind, and he loved me so much. I thought I wanted to be a professor's wife."

Lemon icing coats the top of my mouth. I try to imagine Mom being someone else's wife. I try to imagine being someone else's daughter. The daughter of someone named Herb.

"I met Pops at a party. A rooftop of a penthouse somewhere off Lexington. A party for visiting professors, I think. He was there with his Hasselblad camera covering the event for the school paper."

Mom lifts her cup to her lips. This is the story of my beginning, dripping out in small drops. Each drop leads to who I am.

"I was standing beside the half wall looking over the city—there was a spectacular, vibrant sunset—cadmium orange and ultramarine violet—and Pops walked over and started shooting pictures. Of me. The whirr of the camera nonstop."

Mom. The stylish, elegant movie star.

"Then someone came over to get him to play. They'd set up a trio right there on the rooftop. And he slid behind his drums, never taking his eyes off me while they launched into 'What a Little Moonlight Can Do.'"

Colors and drumbeats. The sun setting. The moon rising. My parents falling in love. How I began.

"At the break, I asked him if he was a photographer or a musician. He said, 'I'm a journalist studying to be a junkie.' I thought it was the funniest thing I'd ever heard. None of those stuffed-shirt professors would have ever said such a thing."

Gray swirls into the corners of the Automat. A story behind this story, like an echo between two buildings. Words I don't know. Questions I don't know how to ask.

"We talked all night. All night under the stars until the sun rose."

Mom's hands are curled around her cup. The steam from the coffee rises up and frames her face, frames the memory.

"There was nothing I could do. You were born," she pauses the space of a breath, a heartbeat, "nine months later. Herb was very decent about it. He ended up marrying another professor, a woman from upstate. Henrietta."

"Henrietta! Herb and Henrietta?"

Mom laughs and the gray swirls are blown away. "There was nothing I could do. You needed to be born. You needed us. Pops and me."

Mom's eyes drop to stare into her coffee. The story evaporates.

I think there is a clue I've missed. I search for it in the words and the colors and the drumbeats, but it's gone. I squish the last crumbs of cake and lick them off my fork.

Making Sense of the World

Pops says the world makes sense through a beat.
He says drumsticks help him to hear.
    Mom says the world makes sense through
the pull and twist of a brush. She says colors
help her to see.

> I make sense of the world with words.
> They rumble deep in my throat.
> I shape them with my lips.
> Sounds swirl on the air into meaning.
>
> Words snake down to the pen in my hand.
> My fingers curl and glide.
> Lines, curves and dots dance on the page.
> I make sense of the world with words.
>
> But sometimes words gray out.
> Sometimes words are a broken time
>   signature.
> Sometimes words won't work.
> Do the words know me better than I know
>   myself?

Coney Island of the Mind

Pops and Ira and I are going to Coney Island.

Not for the hot dogs. Not for the cotton candy.

We're going to Coney Island because of a poet. Lawrence Ferlinghetti.

Pops said if I was going to be a poet, I needed to know about all kinds of poets. Especially Lawrence Ferlinghetti because he lives in California where Pops was born.

"You're an angelheaded hipster," Pops says to me. He's got a copy of Ferlinghetti's book *A Coney Island of the Mind* under his arm.

"You got that right," says Ira.

Pops stands in the middle of the bridge to Coney Island. The wind is slapping my face. He opens the book, spreads his arms and reads Ferlinghetti to the seagulls.

the poet like an acrobat
climbs on rime
to a high wire of his own making"

He dances on the boardwalk, and the loose planks of wood make chiming sounds.

"Hey, Miss Missy, it's a xylophone," says Ira, and we jump from board to board, slapping out the rhythm of the day.

My lips get sticky from saltwater taffy. We all scream on the roller coaster.

Ira wins me a stuffed bear by hitting a target at the shooting range.

"Learned how to shoot in Korea, baby. Ain't nothin' I can't win with the pull of a trigger!"

I bury my face in the bear's soft fur. Bright yellow eyes glow from a sleek black head.

"Call him Mr. Carter," says Ira. "After the man who delivered my momma."

Pops holds his copy of *A Coney Island of the Mind* high in the air and recites to the man at the arcade.

"... *where the world rushes by*
       in a blather of asphalt and delay..."

And even though it sounds sad, he's got the biggest, goofiest smile on his face and I pile mustard and sauerkraut onto my hot dog and we sit on the sand and watch the sun get swallowed by the sea and the lights come on and it's like a fairy tale.

I want to be an angelheaded hipster forever.

It's All About the Words

In the morning, there's a new poem beside my
bed. A Pops poem, Ferlinghetti-style.

> *It's all about the words, honey,*
> *the sound and the beat,*
> *your heart is the beat,*
> *feed your soul with the beat,*
> *your life is your art,*
> *your voice is your heart,*
> *it's what we do.*
> *Me and you.*

It's what we do. Me and you.
I tape it on the wall above my bed.

Mrs. Nault's Sonnet

Mrs. Nault wants us to write a sonnet. I tell her
I'm an angelheaded hipster and want to write a
poem
>> *like Lawrence Ferlinghetti*
>>> *with lines all broken*
>>> *and no rhymes, except in the middle*
>>>> *or by accident.*
> She says I have to write a sonnet first. So I do.
But it's really hard.

A SONNET FOR MRS. NAULT
by Miranda Billie Taylor

You say a sonnet's what I have to write.
With five stressed syllables in every line.
Soft and hard. The beats are called iambs.
They sound just like the beating of my heart.
Da-dum da-dum da-dum da-dum da-dum.
In fourteen lines a sonnet tells a tale.
Haikus and tankas are much easier.
You say to be a poet I must write
Like Shakespeare first, since he's the best
>> *there is.*
You say that every other line should rhyme

But I think that's impossible to do.
Still, I can write a couplet at the end
And make the last two lines so that they
*   rhyme.*
To write a sonnet takes a lot of time.

Live at the Village Vanguard

"Shhh."

Pops is a silhouette in my doorway.

Sleep tugs me down.

"Hurry. I've got a cab waiting."

Pops's voice pulls me up.

My clock says 11:45.

"Look."

In his arms, he's holding...me? I'm still in bed, but he's holding me in his arms. I reach out to touch one of my nightgowns filled with sweaters, cradled to his chest.

"Just in case," he says. "Come on."

I get out of bed. He pulls back the covers and slips in the fake Missy, tucking my still-warm blankets around a still, cold, pretend me.

"Trane is at the Vanguard with Dolphy. They're putting on a late set. I'll wait for you outside."

The Village Vanguard is famous. The best jazz musicians in the world play there.

I'm wide awake and silently pulling clothes from my dresser. Black knit skirt, black turtleneck, black tights. Pull my brush through nighttime tangles. A black headband.

I look in the mirror.

I'm an angelheaded hipster.

The taxi is too hot. Thin traces of rain pattern the windshield. We're streaming through rivers of yellow taxis. Through the night to 7th Avenue. The midnight cold is making goosebumps on my arms.

The taxi stops in front of a long red awning. I stand under it out of the rain while Pops pays the driver. I should have worn a coat.

Pops leads me down the steps into the dark. The ceiling is low, the room like a cave. It's not fancy, not like the Hickory House. There's a small stage at the end of the room with soft red curtains behind it. There's the hum of late-night, like when people are over for the music at home. Quiet talk and the ting of ice cubes in glasses. Waiters carry trays filled with drinks.

Pops heads to the only free table, behind a pillar. I sit on the bench. I can hardly see the stage.

"If we'd gotten here sooner, we'd have a better seat." He tips his seat back for a better view. "Double Scotch on the rocks. Neat. Shirley Temple," he says to the waiter without looking up.

I watch the waiter work his way through the room, taking orders, filling them at the bar, and then setting them down in front of each customer. I imagine his job, working here night after night, hearing the greatest jazz musicians in the world, watching people come and go.

I smile at him when he brings our drinks, but I'm invisible.

"Cheers, Princess." Pops lifts his glass. "You're going to see history here tonight, honey, history in the making. Trane recorded here in '61, with Dolphy, but Dolphy hasn't played with him in a year. He wasn't supposed to play tonight. But he will. He will." Pops downs his drink, signals the waiter for another.

Names and dates. Names and dates I need to know. More important than anything I learn at school.

I sip my drink slowly but like I mean it. Like I like it. But I don't think Shirley Temples are the drinks of angelheaded hipsters.

The applause rises from the heart of the full room like a wave, greeting the band as they come through the curtains onto the stage. I watch Pops watching them as they adjust their instruments. I wish I could see what he sees. I wish I could hear what he hears.

Light cymbals begin, tA-tda-tda-tA-tda-tda beside a light snare drum.

I look over at Pops. Every part of his body is there, in the beats, in the notes. The bass eases in, joined by the piano. I know there's a story in the music, but I can't find it.

A musician is swaying, eyes shut, a long soprano sax dangling in his hands. When it seems like the drums can't hold on anymore, he eases his sax in like a snake charmer.

This must be Trane. He runs notes run up and down until the man with the alto sax—he must be Dolphy—starts to play. And through it all, the drums hold them solid.

"Jones is a monster," whispers Pops. His hands are twitching. It's like he's playing the drums with Jones. Swishing his brushes, flicking his wrists.

I try to hear, but I don't. Not the way Pops hears. But I close my eyes and suddenly remember going to a restaurant with Mom and Pops. An Indian restaurant down in a basement, with rich and spicy smells like faraway stories. The music is just like that. Like the taste and the smell all mixed together.

The soprano sax—Trane—takes off like a wild bird trying to find its way out of a cage.

It's a long set. I think I must have slept a bit because I jump when the final applause comes.

Lights come up and chairs shift and people start putting on their coats.

Pops heads for the stage. I see him talking to Trane, to Dolphy, to Jones. I can't hear them, but I can see them laughing. Pops turns and waves at me, a finger in the air, nods a just-a-minute look and disappears behind the curtain with the band.

So I wait.

All around me soft voices. People leaving.

I watch the waiter move from table to table collecting glasses, settling bills.

Pops's four empty glasses are lined up across the table. My cherry stem sits in my glass. I lace my fingers together under the table and wait, watching the curtains.

Soon I'm the only one left in the room, other than the waiter.

He picks up the glasses and the ashtray and looks at me like he's seeing me for the first time.

He waits. Is he expecting me to pay the bill?

"I...my father went with Trane and Dolphy. And Jones. To the back." I try to sound as grown-up as possible.

He turns and weaves through the maze of empty tables and chairs to slip through the back curtain.

I wait. I count syllables for a new tanka.
Trane, Dolphy and Jones. (Five.)
Make sounds to tell a story. (Seven.)
Listen hard to hear. (Five.)

And then they come out. Pops, Trane, Dolphy and Jones. Smiling. Trane and Dolphy start packing their horns, Jones his kit.

Finally, Pops looks at me and jerks his head toward the door.

I get up to follow him.

As I pass the waiter, I ask him, loudly, "Can you please tell me what time it is?"

"Two in the morning."

"Two in the morning," I say to the almost empty room.

I want to prove that I'm here. Here in the night, a night of history in the making. I want the waiter to remember me, to see how special it is that I am here, to see how special Pops is for bringing me here, even though Pops is already out on the street, hailing a taxi.

In the taxi I count syllables for two more lines. I repeat the poem over and over in my head so that I can remember it and give it to Pops tomorrow.

TANKA FOR THE VANGUARD
by Miranda Billie Taylor

Trane, Dolphy and Jones
Make sounds to tell a story
Listen hard to hear
History in the making.
Live at the Village Vanguard.

Ira Keeps Us Dry

Ira is waiting outside the school with Pops. It's raining, pouring, and Ira's holding a trash-can lid above their heads.

I don't have an umbrella, so I'm extra happy to see them.

"Come along, Miss Missy. You don't want to be gettin' wet!"

I scoot under the trash-can lid. The rain makes music on the lid and Ira does his Mr. Bojangles dance, so I do a hop-step dance, and we've each got an arm hooked with Pops and we're singing in the rain.

"It's raining, it's pouring. The old man is snoring."

It's Thursday and Pops is having one of his bad days. Ira says that can happen after a night of history in the making.

It's Thursday and Mom's at the studio, and Pops is having a bad day, stumbling a bit on the curb while Ira is keeping us dry.

It's Thursday and Ira and I are singing and dancing to remind Pops how to walk.

It's Thursday and we're dancing under the trash-can lid and tomorrow Pops will be fine.

Sunday Afternoon at Willard's

Mom's at her class. Ira's with his girlfriend.

"Her name's Faith, Miss Missy," he told me. "I just know you're gonna love her. I'll be bringing her round next Sunday. Just you wait."

Late slanting sunlight, and Pops is taking me to his friend Willard's. We walk up the steps of a large building on Grand Street, above a bridal shop. Pops pushes open the door. Smells spin out and coat me. Oil paint like at Mom's studio. Musty wet, like an old facecloth. Sweet smoke mixed with cigarette smoke, and something that makes me think of pigeons. The outside daylight streams in through tall grime-colored windows, catching curls of smoke trails and making dust specks sparkle in the air.

I've never been to church, but this makes me feel like I should pray to someone or something.

"Converted synagogue," says Pops, as though he's read my mind.

Enormous painted canvases line the wooden walls. Huge swashes of midnight black and ultramarine. Colors like a noisy conversation, or maybe an argument.

At the far end, on a raised platform, there's

a piano, an upright honky-tonk. Stand-up bass. Drum kit, high hat, cymbals.

And in the middle of this huge space with ceilings as tall as a giant, in the inside of this converted synagogue over a bridal shop on Grand Street...there's a tiny house. Flowered curtains, a small wooden door. A storybook house.

Pops strides over to it, flourishes his drumsticks and taps out a paradiddle around the doorframe. Par-a-did-dle. Par-a-did-dle. Par-a-did-dle. Par-a-did-dle.

Inside the house inside the house, I hear someone laugh. It sounds like a little girl.

"Willard, my man." Pops's grin is wide.

"Captain." Willard emerges from the house, grabbing Pops's hand in a familiar shake. With his tight beard and a mass of brown curls, Willard looks like one of the Seven Dwarfs.

Suddenly a tiny face pops between Willard's legs and smiles at Pops.

"Capt'n!"

"Hey, Sarah, flip me some skin."

Sarah holds her hand out. Slap, pull, flip. Slap, pull, flip.

I've never seen her before, but she knows Pops.

"Sarah, this is my daughter Missy."

Sarah's got long lashes that blink twice. A

question moves across her face but then she smiles. She holds out her hand.

"Flip me some skin," she says in a little voice. So I do. Slap, pull, flip. Slap, pull, flip.

At the last flip she grabs my hand. "We're finger painting!" She squeals and pulls me into the storybook house, covering my hands in a soft greasy squish of primary red, the color of a cartoon apple. Swish, sklunch, shlapp. Her hands spread color over thin paper.

"Who do you think ith comin' to town? You'll never gueth who! Lovable, huggable Emily Brown. Mith Brown to you!" She sings loudly, through missing front teeth, swaying and slapping her paint-drenched fingers on the paper.

Outside the storybook house, I hear instruments tested, tuned. Pops's brushes are sliding over the drum skins, tapping the high hat. I can feel the vibration of the bass tuck into the beat. The drums and bass set the pace, the piano eases in, the story starts —

"I'm hungry."

Sarah's whine pierces through the sax solo. Red paint is starting to dry and flake on her face.

There's the trumpet now, cold clear notes hitting the worn walls of the old synagogue.

"I'm hungry."

I suddenly realize this is why I'm here. I'm supposed to look after Sarah so the band can play in peace. I want to be here for the music.

I want to keep my mind on the drums, listen for the swish of Pops's brushes.

"I thaid I'm hungry!"

I run water in the storybook sink and our fingers slide and grab at soap bubbles, the water pink.

"I can hop to fifthy," says Sarah on one leg. "One, two three, four…" There's a doll-sized refrigerator with just enough peanut butter and jelly and crackers. "Thirthy. Thirthy-one."

I listen for the new beat — 7/8. I spread peanut butter, then jelly, on crackers. The energy picks up and the sax is wailing, crying, the trumpet chasing him, then the drums beating them both back, taking their solo, turning the world upside down like a runaway horse galloping across Times Square.

I find a doll-sized plate and hand Sarah the four crackers. I look out the window of the little house into the bigger one and see Pops, his hands a blur with the speed of his sticks. Every part of him is the sound.

"I want a thtory." Sara tugs my hand and pulls me over to a tiny bed.

I want to hit her.

She hands me a paint-speckled copy of the Brothers Grimm. I crawl onto the bed beside her.

"Once upon a time in the middle of winter, when the snowflakes were falling like feathers from the sky, a queen sat at her window working, and her embroidery frame was of ebony..."

I guess I fall asleep because suddenly the music stops and my eyes snap open. Sarah's sweaty head is heavy on my arm. I slide out slowly. She sucks her thumb fiercely but doesn't wake up.

Outside the little house it's dark now. Light from huge candles flicker reflections in the windows. The paintings only peep through the shadows through the smoke curls.

Pops and his friends are all at the other end of the synagogue sitting in the candlelight, the tips of their cigarettes glowing.

If I could sing, I could be part of their world. In my head I hear Billie, always. I want to open my mouth and have her sound glide out. I imagine striding over and singing *"Who do you think is comin' to town? You'll never guess who..."* as I reach for a cigarette.

But I know my voice doesn't sound like Billie's. Not really. Not when it's outside of me.

And it's Sunday and I have a project on Jupiter to finish for school tomorrow.

It's Sunday and I'm supposed to study my French verbs.

It's Sunday and I'm supposed to get to bed early.

Je dors. Je dormais. J'ai dormi. Je dormirai. Je dormirais.

I am sleeping. I was sleeping. I have slept. I will sleep. I would sleep.

They drift back to their instruments, their eyes and ears only for the music. I watch Pops settle behind the drums, pick up his sticks, test and tighten the skins.

I feel like a ghost, the ghost of the synagogue.

"Pops?"

I say it quietly. Rule number one. Don't make Pops mad. Rule number two. Don't interrupt.

But it's Sunday and I'm hungry.

"Pops?"

I say it a bit louder, as the notes start to bounce into the space and begin to fill it. I'm breaking the rules, but I have to go home.

"Pops."

It's like I've hurled a box of glass Christmas ornaments from the rooftop, the crash sending shards through the scene.

They all stop and stare at me.

"I need to go home."

My voice sounds pathetic, worse than Sarah.

In two strides Pops is in front of me and I'm frozen.

"Don't. Do. That. Again. Ever."

"Do what?"

"Embarrass me like that." He shoves a ten-dollar bill at me. "Take a cab."

And he goes back to his stool, picks up his sticks. He starts into the opening drum solo of "Billie's Bounce."

Don't. Do. That. Again. Ever.

I walk out of the dancing light of the synagogue, away from the swirling sax solo, away from the storybook house and Sarah and the world inside a world inside a world, and into gray drizzle. I hail a cab. Pops taught me how when I was four. "In case of emergencies," he'd said. But I don't need to do it on my own very often.

"525, East 14th Street. Stuyvesant Town."

It's Sunday. After dinner, maybe Mom and I can watch *Bonanza*. If she's home. If she's home, I hope we can have something nice for dinner. Something that isn't peanut butter and jelly.

Pops Writes Me a Song

I find it in the morning beside my bed, with a broken white shell on top.

I know it's a song because he has drawn musical notes beside the words.

> *Just you and me — in the country*
> *Where grass isn't made to*
> *Be lawn-like,*
> *Baby deer aren't afraid to*
> *Be fawn-like and*
> *You'd carry on*
> *Like a natural child would do.*
> *"Thou didst smile,*
> *Infused with a fortitude from heaven."*

I know it's a special song just for me, because of the line that Prospero says to Miranda, a line that Pops wrote out when I was born, a line that is tacked above my bed.

Thou didst smile,
Infused with a fortitude from heaven.

I know his song means more than the words *I'm sorry*. I put the broken shell and the song in my heart-shaped treasure box.

I don't see Pops for a few days. Mom says Double Life World can be a busy place.

Rebound and Collision

I'm broken out of sleep by a hard-hitting drum solo, the kind that whacks the tom-tom, zings the high hat, pitches off the ride cymbal and wails on the snare. A solo that's a midnight sound, not a seven-in-the-morning sound.

I look for Mom. She's in their bedroom. Pops's pale blue laundered shirts are in an open suitcase, wrapped in tissue and folded onto cardboard. Mom rolls a navy silk tie and tucks it into the corner. Her hands look like they aren't sure they want to be there. I see a smear of gray paint on her wrist.

"Pops is going to Florida." Her voice sounds like a rusty door handle. "They've asked him to speak at the American Association of Magazine Photographers annual convention. It is a great honor."

Da-Da-Da-Ching. Da-Da-Da-Ching. Da-Da-Da-Ching. Da-Da-Da-Ching.

Rapid-fire drum sounds squish us into the room.

Every space in the apartment is filled with a jagged beat.

"If it's an honor, then why isn't he happy to

go?" Even I know what Pops's drum solo is saying.

Mom packs Pops's brush and comb. "He hates public speaking. He hates being looked at. He's the man behind the camera, not the man in the picture."

The man behind the drum kit, not the front man.

"Why?"

"The association loved the photos he took at the Democratic Convention in 1960. Award-winning photos. Photos of history in the making. Amazing."

"No, I mean why does Pops hate being looked at?"

Mom tucks four pairs of black socks into the suitcase pocket. "It was his mother. He says that when he was a boy, she stared at him all the time. Kept saying he was so beautiful. She went on and on about his beautiful long eyelashes. So when he was twelve, he cut them off."

"Twelve? Like me? He cut off his eyelashes?!"

Mom slowly closes and latches the case. "He told me he thought it was the only way to shut her up. The only way to make her stop looking at him. At least, that's how he tells the story."

She scoops the suitcase off the bed, and I follow her down the hall. I feel the warmth of her shoulder as we stand together, watching.

Pops is a wild blur. Sweat flies through the air as his head and arms flash from side to side, hitting drum skins, rims, sides, stand, foot pedal, high hat, cymbal, bell — hitting everything.

This is what Pops has told me about drumming: "It's all about rebound and control, honey."

Rebound and control.

I looked them up in the dictionary.

Rebound: To spring back on collision or impact with another body.

Control: To check or regulate, to exercise restraining influence over.

I wonder if cutting off your eyelashes is rebound and control.

Lady Murasaki on Stage

Pops is away and Mom says it's all right for Corky to stay overnight. We're going to work on her costume for the end-of-year show. The theme is Japan and Japanese culture. Mrs. Nault has given Corky the lead role. Lady Murasaki.

"But I thought Japanese women had black hair."

I'm a little jealous. I don't mean to be but I am. Lady Murasaki is the star of the show and Corky's hair is white blonde.

"We'll paint mine black on the day of the show," says Corky.

"Japanese women don't have breasts," I point out. Corky wears a bra because she needs one. I wear one because she does.

"We'll bind me up," laughs Corky.

When Corky's happy she has all the answers.

Corky's mom, Gerry, bought fabric from the Five and Dime. Swirls of cadmium orange and scarlet. I hold one end and Corky spins into it until she's all tied up.

Pin and trim. Tie and knot. Ultramarine waves with splashes of white foam crash across

Corky's back. Silver and manganese-blue fish dance on her arms.

She pushes white socked feet into flip-flop sandals. She takes tiny tight steps, sits on the floor and arranges herself to look like the painting in the book. She holds the paper fan Gerry got for her, decorated with a painting of a snow-covered mountain.

She puts her smile away. Her face is calm and a bit sad.

She's a good actress. Even with her blonde hair I have to admit she's a perfect Lady Murasaki.

"You like it when you're on stage, don't you? You like being the star."

She picks her chin up and looks at me. "Is there something wrong with that?"

"Not everyone does."

"I know. But I love it."

Corky looks at an imaginary audience and quotes from the play.

"But though hers may have been the greater grief we must not think that there was not at that moment very deep emotion on both sides."

She looks so serious and sad that I can't help laughing.

Mom comes in with a tray. There are two tiny cups painted with blue flowers. She bows low to Corky and sets the tray on the floor. "Green tea. If you look closely, you can see grains of rice inside the china."

The tea is bitter and smells like wet leaves in November.

"If my mother had known about *The Tale of Genji*," Corky says, "maybe she would have named me Murasaki. Or maybe just Saki. Then we'd be Miranda and Saki."

Stan curls up on Corky's lap. Ollie glares from Pops's chair.

A TANKA FOR LADY MURASAKI
by Miranda Billie Taylor and
Courtney Fisher

In the soft moonlight
Lady Murasaki fans
Herself and writes poems. (Missy)
Beside her sits her best friend.
Together they drink their tea. (Corky)

Mono No Aware

Mrs. Nault gives me lines to say at the end-of-year play. I get to say them at the very end, like an epilogue, says Mrs. Nault. That means they are important. Beginnings and endings are important.

My lines explain why Lady Murasaki wrote *The Tale of Genji*. I don't get to wear a special costume like Corky, but it's an important part of the story.

> MISSY: Lady Murasaki wrote the phrase *Mono no aware* over one thousand times in *The Tale of Genji*. *Mono no aware* means the fragility of life. The sorrow of human existence.
> *Mono no aware* means a gentle sadness, a wistfulness about the fleeting nature of life. Impermanence is the reality of life.
> *Mono no aware*.

On the Day Pops Comes Home from Florida

I let myself into Apartment 5D after school. Pops is pacing.

> Mom is at her job and Pops is pacing.
> Pacing in the apartment.
> Writing on a pad of yellow paper.
> Pacing.
> In 5D.
>
> Pops is mumbling.
> There is no one in the room.
> He is not talking to me.
> He doesn't know I am there.
> He is murmuring.
> Words not meant for me.
>
> Louder now, demanding.
> His steps unrhythmic slaps.
> His hands jab anger.
> The room echoes back.
>
> My back is pressed against the door.
> The knob grinds my spine.

Slowly I reach behind and hold the smooth
round cool in my hand.

I turn it silently.

And go downstairs to Apartment 4D.

I can do my homework at Corky's.

Not Talking

Pops doesn't go to *Pepsi-Cola World* anymore.
Pops sleeps on the couch during the day.
When he is there, I have to be quiet.
He wears dark glasses. And a ski jacket.
In June.
Even when he is sleeping.

Pops's ski jacket is puffy and red—vermilion.
Pops's ski pants are shiny and black—coal.
Pops wears his ski clothes everywhere.
And he's started smoking a cigar.

Pops's cigar is wet where he chews it.
Pops's cigar smells sweet and heavy and cold.
Sometimes fat piles of ashes fall on the ice in
    his drink.
Pops carries his drink everywhere.

Pops makes notes on pads of paper—cadmium
    lemon.
Pops makes notes when other people talk.
Pops makes big arrows with a fat marker.
Pops carries his clipboard everywhere.

Since Pops came back from the conference, he doesn't talk to me anymore.

Mom Tells Me New Rules

Missy, you need to be quiet.
    You must not ask questions
    Or worse, disagree.
    Do not say no.

    Missy, you need to be small.
    No sudden noises
    Or worse, a surprise.
    Always say yes.

    Make him feel safe.
    Use very few words.
    Please do your best.
    Remember the rules.

The Day Everything Started to Change

Pops is fixing his bicycle.

There are bicycle parts scattered over the floor of the living room. His drum brushes are taped to the handlebars. The soft metal fans of the brushes look set to catch the rhythm of the road.

Mom is standing still, watching.

Pops's cigarette is stuck in his ear. It sticks out sideways like a flag. But it's not lit.

Beside his bike there's:

> a box of tapes, reel-to-reels, the ones where the tape stretches around a big disk
>
> a pile of his clothes, all of his favorites, white jeans and black turtlenecks
>
> a big box of books with titles like *Being and Nothingness*
>
> two bottles of his favorite Scotch, J&B, full.

"We're going to California, Princess." He rubs the bike chain with a greasy cloth. "You'll ride on the back."

Ice cubes tinkle in his glass.

I look at all of the things stacked beside the bike, the things he is planning to take. Boxes of clothes and books. Scotch and reel-to-reel tapes.

And me. On his bike. To California.

Mom's voice is squished, quiet. "That's a long way to go on a bicycle."

Pops tightens a nut on the brake pad.

"I'm not leaving her here with you." His voice is low, growling. Dangerous.

There's a jagged crackle in the air.

Remember the rules.

The eternity of the next second passes. No surprises, no sudden noises. I am as small as I can be.

Mom's voice tiptoes slowly. "It's time for Missy to go to school."

She is looking at Pops, but she's talking to me. I feel her hands tighten on my shoulders. My feet move as she turns me toward the door. Slow motion, as she closes the door behind me with a soft click.

Corky is in the lobby with Patty. She says words but I don't talk. On the street the traffic sounds like ocean waves. I watch people ride past on their bicycles.

Not one has drum brushes on the handles.

Not one has reel-to-reel tapes, a box of books, clothes and J&B Scotch strapped on.

Not one has a girl like me riding on the back.

Saying No

Mom picks me up after school. Rumbling trucks and demanding car horns fill the spaces between us.

We go to Al's Diner. I order a grilled cheese sandwich, my favorite, and dip it in sticky ketch-up. I chew a bit of the edge. But I'm not hungry.

I'm afraid of Mom's face, a face of glass.

The rules mean I can't say no to Pops. Can I say no to Mom? Is Mom part of the new rules?

"I don't want to go to California on a bicycle."

Mom is still for a very long time. Her cof-fee cup is full, but she doesn't drink it. There's a greasy slick over the creamy surface. She's look-ing at the cup, but I don't think she sees it.

I forget I'm not supposed to tear up my nap-kin. It looks like snow under the table.

"You aren't going to California on a bicycle, honey," Mom says. She looks out the window.

There's a tear beside Mom's nose.

I have so many questions. *You must not ask questions.*

I give her a piece of my torn napkin.

I don't know what else to do.

Pops Leaves a New Poem

The bike and boxes and tapes and clothes wait silently in the living room. There's a poem beside my bed, with a gray pebble on top.

> *Her smile has the*
> *power*
> *of seagulls*
> *to lull*
> *drowning monkeys.*
> *Never melt,*
> *snowball heart.*
> *What is this thing with us medicine men?*
> *Certainly we cannot blame witchcraft itself.*
> *Only thing to do is*
> *START AGAIN*
> *we've been saving all*
> *these pretty words*
> *NOBODY CAN'T STILL USE!*

I put the gray pebble in my special heart-shaped treasure box. I put the paper in my heart-shaped box. For later. Maybe later I'll understand.

I know some poems are like that.

Names and Arrows Pointing Nowhere

Tuesday, after school. The door isn't locked.

I push gently. No sudden noises, no surprises. It takes two deep breaths until my eyes see through the gloom. I take small steps, so silent my ears hurt from the beat of my pulse.

He's not there.

Full ashtrays, empty glasses. The couch covered in papers. Papers from the yellow pad. Papers thick on the table, on the floor, taped to the windows. Papers blocking out the light.

I move in closer.

Names and arrows cover the papers. Charts and names and arrows. Names I know—Ira, Elaine, Barry, Willard, and me, Miranda, and Mom, Jean. Names I don't know but have heard—Isabel, BJ, Dr. F.

Arrows. Dates. Times. Words.

And scribbled in huge letters, one word per page, five pages taped to a different wall:

WORDS   NOBODY   CAN'T
STILL   USE

I make myself invisible and slip out the door of 5D.

Outside, the air is soft. If I walk long enough, Mom will come home, and the papers will be gone. If I walk long enough, the words I don't understand won't be there.

Tomorrow Begins

Pops's voice cracks from the living room into my sleep, my dreams, my middle of the night.

"You're on their side." His words flung like a drum solo out of control, demanding attention. "You're one of them!" Rat-tat-a-tat. Rat-tat-a-tat. Rebounding off the living-room walls. "I'm not leaving her here with you!" Sharp, crisp.

He means me. Not leaving me here with Mom.

Suddenly he's filling my doorway, backlit, a silhouette. He's a bear in a vermilion ski jacket, breathing fire through the gleam of his cigar

"Get dressed. Now!"

There is no carriage, no horse, no fake Missy to leave in my place.

Mom is behind him. Her voice toneless.

"Paul, it's two in the morning. Let her get ready tomorrow. Let her go back to sleep."

"No. She can't stay here with you another minute. We're leaving NOW!"

Fire and ice flood my body.

But then Ira comes into the doorway, like he's walking onto a stage.

"Hey, brother, let's let Miss Missy have her

98 | THESE ARE NOT THE WORDS

beauty sleep. Let's head uptown. They're waitin'
for us uptown."

I blink and they are gone. I blink and the
doorframe holds only Mom.

I blink and tomorrow begins.

4D at Two in the Morning

I'm in my nightie. The stairwell is a hard metal echo. Mom is taking me downstairs. The stairs, not the elevator.

4D. Words with soft edges. Bare feet cold on the linoleum as I cross the familiar territory to an unfamiliar bed on the couch. Corky and Patty in their room, asleep.

Light from the kitchen spilling onto the couch. Whispers drifting. In my hands, Corky's favorite mug, the one with the blue Japanese mountain. Cinnamon steam rises from the snow-covered peak.

The glowing clock on the windowsill says 3:35.

The streetlight outside makes shadows. The hairs on my knees prickle under my chin. I hold my legs curled tight.

In the morning there are sweet warm smells from the kitchen. I hear Gerry go down the hall to wake Corky and Patty.

I wait. I hear sounds but no words. I pretend I am asleep.

"Missy?"

Gerry's hand is on my shoulder. Corky and

Patty are beside her. Their faces full of we're-not-allowed-to-ask-you-any-questions.

Gerry hands me clothes. I open my eyes and recognize Corky's skirt and white blouse, ankle socks and scuffed Buster Brown shoes.

Gerry's voice sounds like she's in a play. "Get dressed quickly. All of you. I've made pancakes."

"Pancakes?" says Corky. "It's Wednesday."

"A breakfast party," says Gerry.

"Why?" says Patty.

"Why not?" says Gerry.

The syrup is cold and the butter doesn't melt and my throat doesn't want to swallow. Patty spills juice and has to change. Corky lets me use her toothbrush. Gerry braids my hair too tight and my eyes water.

Corky waits until the lobby to ask.

"Why did you sleep at our place?"

I shrug.

"What did your mom say?"

"Nothing."

"She must have said something."

I look straight ahead.

"Your mom just brought you down to sleep on our couch in your nightgown, in the middle of the night, and she said nothing?"

Patty starts jumping up and down. "I bet they

THESE ARE NOT THE WORDS | 101

had a fight. I bet Missy's mom and dad are going to get a divorce like our mom and dad. Then you get two places to live!"

Corky walks in front of me, backwards. I smell the toothpaste on her breath. I'm watching my feet. "*Did* they have a fight?"

I'm not leaving her here with you.

Corky waits, then spins around. At the red light she takes Patty's hand. The light changes and they walk together.

I listen to the sound of my shoes, Corky's too-big shoes, on the sidewalk. Flop. Flop. Flop. I slow down and break them into a two-beat. Thunk-flop. Thunk-flop. Thunk-flop. Thunk-flop. I don't need to look up to know how to get to school.

Corky and Patty don't wait.

On the Day When Nothing Is Said

After school I unlock 5D, because it is what I do. The apartment is heavy with quiet.

My eardrums thud with emptiness.

"Hello?"

Pops's chair twisted over. Drumsticks and brushes on the floor. The TV on, the sound off. Curtains drawn against the sun.

Stan winds around my legs, impatient to be fed. I reach down and pick her up. But she leaps out of my arms, pushing off with her hind legs, scratching my chest through Corky's blouse.

"Ow!!! Stupid cat!" I yell it as loud as I can to fill the empty apartment with sound.

Stan comes back to rub against my legs and I swat her away with the side of my hand. She streaks under the couch.

Ollie glares at me from Pops's chair.

The scratch stings and I can see little beads of blood bubbling up. I grab a tissue from the box on Pops's table so that my blood doesn't get on Corky's blouse.

The phone rings and I jump.

"Hey, Miss Missy."

"Ira!"

"I don' have much time, honey. You gotta tell your momma your Captain Daddy Pops won't let me near him. I can't do it. He can't abide me bein' 'round him. You gotta tell her."

"Can you come over?"

"I can't come over. He don't trust me right now. He hears I been there, he's gonna get worse."

"But Ira—"

"You gotta be strong, Miss Missy. You gotta look after your momma. She loves that man too much, too hard. An' she can't fix this. It's too much."

"Ira, I'm scared—"

"Don't you be cryin' Miss Missy. Your Captain Daddy Pops loves his Missy, but he's goin' through a bad spell. I'm gonna make sure he's okay but you gotta look after yourself. Look after your momma. Trust your momma. Be strong."

Dial tone.

I put the receiver down.

I pick it up again. Still a dial tone. I slam it down as hard as I can and Ollie streaks under the couch.

Ira's supposed to be here.

The stale tang of cigar smoke hangs like a heavy blanket. *I Love Lucy* flickers silently on the TV.

I pick up Pops's drum brush and flick it across

my palm. Swish-slap, swish-slap. Soft. Calling. Like a story.

I try to swish-slap and sing the song Mom and Pops and I used to sing together when I was little.

"Oh, we ain't got a barrel of money,
Maybe we're ragged and funny
But we'll travel along
Singing a song..."

5D sounds even more empty.

I lock the door and take the stairs down to Apartment 4D. Gerry asks Corky and me to help make dinner. Spaghetti with fish cakes. She doesn't notice Corky not speaking to me.

When Mom phones 4D, there are sounds behind her. A crowded room. Strange beeps. Pinging.

"You're going to need to spend the night at Corky's."

There's no music, no time signature to her words.

My throat is tight. "Stan scratched me..."

Remember the rules. No sudden noises.

I swallow. "Ira called. He said Pops won't let him near. He said I need to look after you." I try to understand the mechanical sounds behind her.

"I'm fine. Don't worry." It's hard not to worry

when Ira and Mom tell me not to worry. "Everything is going to be all right, but I need you to stay at Corky's. Go up and feed the cats, and then stay at Corky's. I'll see you after school tomorrow. I'll pick you up. At school."

Gerry sends Corky and me to the pizza man on Avenue A for our favorite treat—tiny paper cups of lemon ice.

I can tell Corky's mad at me. We promised we'd never have secrets from each other unless they were good secrets like about Christmas or birthdays. But I don't have the right words. I don't know all the rules.

Her mouth makes a big noise as she sucks the lemon ice off the wooden spoon. My mouth takes small tastes. We walk back to #525.

In the elevator she pushes 4. I push 5.

In 5D, I switch on the light. Stan and Ollie lift identical heads from the couch. Their blue eyes follow me as I lift Pops's chair and set it upright. I place his sticks and brushes on his desk. I turn off the TV. I empty the ashtray. I carry his glass to the sink, wash it, dry it, put it away.

I get a large scoop of cat food and clatter it into their dish. I hear them drop onto the floor and patter into the kitchen. They don't look at me. They only want food.

How can I look after things if I don't know what is going on? How can I look after Mom if I can't find her?

Ira—tell me what to do!

The phone doesn't ring.

I go to my bedroom and take out the overnight bag I never use. I'm moving underwater. There are no sounds on the ocean floor. I pack my nightgown and clean underwear. Open the drawers of my dresser. Look at clothes. Color hurts my eyes. I pull out gray socks, gray sweater, gray skirt. Fossil gray. I go to the bathroom and get my toothbrush.

The phone doesn't ring.

Stan and Ollie are washing each other in the hall. They race under the couch as soon as they see me.

At the front door, I turn off the light and 5D disappears.

I close and lock the door.

The stillness squishes me into a jagged lump of coal. I trail dust through the hall, down the stairwell, down to the open door of 4D.

It's Hard to Explain

Mom and I are at Al's, beside the window. There's a grilled cheese sandwich between us. But I'm not hungry. And I guess Mom isn't either.

"I had to take Pops to the hospital."

Al refills Mom's coffee cup. I watch a drip slide past Mom's scarlet lipstick stain and down into the saucer.

"Is he okay?"

"He will be."

The words sound like an escalator going down.

"Can I go see him?"

"No." Mom snaps the word and it shuts like a change purse.

"Can Ira go see him?"

"No. The doctor says we shouldn't see him right now."

Mom is fiddling with the short fat cup. It makes a sound like scooping sand as she turns it in the saucer.

"How long will he be in the hospital?"

"I don't know, honey."

"What's *wrong* with him?"

"It's hard to explain."

I stare at my hands in my lap. Bits of my

shredded napkin are clinging to my skirt. There's a snowman's worth of torn napkin at my feet. I don't hear anything except Mom's breathing. The edge of the table is a grimy metal strip. I scrape my finger along the ridge but stop at a nail where there's a sticky red patch. Dried ketchup. I do it again. Scrape, stop. Scrape, stop. Gooey red is piling up under my fingernail.

Mom clears her throat so that I look at her.

"After we were married, Pops's mother told me he'd had psychotic episodes when he was a teenager. Paranoia. It meant that he had . . . times when he was scared. Scared of other people. He didn't trust anybody. She took him to the hospital for treatment called electroshock therapy. They zapped his brain with electricity."

Suddenly there are a lot of words. I can't hold them all in my head.

I hear Pops was sick when he was a teenager. I hear he was scared. I hear his mother took him to the hospital.

"She told me it had worked. He told me it had made him lose parts of his memory. He said there was an emptiness. He couldn't fill it." Mom's ragged breath falls across the table. "He said he'd make new memories with me. With you. He said we could fill the holes."

Mom is looking past me out the window to the street. I try to see what she sees. Late afternoon sun is glinting off an oil puddle beside the curb. The gutter has a rainbow in it.

I have to be still. I have to let Mom say things I don't want to hear.

A car drives through the puddle and the rainbow colors swirl. I watch them settle again.

I hear Mom's cup scrape the saucer. "I thought he was joking when he said he was a journalist studying to be a junkie. I didn't know he was taking junk to fill the holes. By the time I found out, it was too late."

"Junk?"

"Heroin. Junk, dope, smack, snow." Her mouth twists with words that screech like metal wheels on subway rails.

What is this thing with us medicine men?

Certainly we cannot blame witchcraft itself.

A story under the story.

"He says it helps him hear the music. He thinks the junk and the booze cancel each other out. Junk brings him up, booze brings him down. But none of it is real. He's addicted to them both. He's trying to cover the fear."

"Why is Pops afraid?"

She looks at me. I wait. It doesn't matter that

I don't understand the words. I need to hear her say them.

"When his brain gets sick, he gets anxious. Paranoid. Scared of everyone and everything. Florida brought on an attack and he needed more junk to fill bigger holes."

The sounds falling from her lips are like boulders. I push a wedge of sandwich into the ketchup but don't eat it. These are not the words I want. These words are not Pops.

Mom spins her cup around slowly, holding it by the handle. Around and around, the sandy sound filling the space between us.

"They are going to try the electroshock therapy again."

The words bump in my head. Pile on each other. I sort through them, put them in a line. There's something that doesn't fit.

"Doesn't that mean he'll lose more memories?"

Mom looks at me the way Dr. Kildare on the TV show looks at a patient when he tells them bad news.

"It's a chance we have to take."

A chance we have to take.

I suddenly realize what Mom means. Pops might lose memories of us. Of me.

"No!" I have to stop this. "He doesn't want to.

I know he doesn't want to!" I feel as though Pops and I are on two sides of a raging river and I've got to save him. "He'll drown!"

Mom's face is like a drawbridge on a castle. Closed. With sharp spikes sticking out.

"No, you can't do this to him!" I'm scraping torn napkin bits from my lap. I've got to get out of Al's.

"Missy—"

"I don't want him to forget!" Christmases at China Boy. Family Portrait. The Hickory House. The Vanguard. Coney Island. Angelheaded hipsters. "Please..."

"He needs help. He's very sick and this is the only way to help him get better."

All of the words fall onto the table. I look at them, shuffle them. "But if he loses more memories, he'll want more drugs to fill bigger holes."

Her cup is empty. She drinks the air.

"The doctors want to try him on a different drug. After the shock therapy. A safe one. Methadone. To make him well."

The drawbridge of Mom's face opens a crack. A bridge that opens up over a crashing river, a bridge of hope.

"But he has to take it." Her voice shrinks the world to the space between us. "He has to *want* to take it. Only he can make that choice."

A choice. If it's a choice, he can get better.

I need to go home, even though Pops won't be there. I need to go home where the TV is on with no sound, where Pops's empty glass sits beside a full ashtray.

"Can I sleep at home tonight?"

Mom reaches across the table and holds my hand.

"We need to be strong."

A POEM FOR POPS WHO IS SICK
by Miranda Billie Taylor

You're sick, but I can't understand what is
    wrong.
You're sick, and I know I've got to be strong.
I miss your paradiddles on the living room
    wall,
Stan and Ollie just yowl and won't settle at
    all.
The apartment's not right when we're here
    and you're not.
Please get well soon. We miss you a lot.

It's a terrible poem. I tear it into the tiniest fragments, then open the window and let it go.

I watch each word, letter, curve, line and comma float away.

I don't want this poem in my life.

Patience

The stone lion on the left side of the steps of the New York Public Library is named Patience. She looks as gentle as a sleeping lion can. I walk up the steps and stretch out my arm to pat her tail.

Pops brought me here last year. He showed me which bus to take along 14th Street, and which subway to take to get to Grand Central station. He showed me the walk across 42nd Street to 5th Avenue.

"If you ever want to know something, you can find it here. This is where to come for answers," he said. "It's the safest, quietest place in the whole city."

There are flowering linden trees outside the library. I know the name because Pops told me. His father lives on a street called Linden Street in California. But we have nothing to do with him. I like the sweet smell, though. It makes me think of Mom's perfume.

Inside, the library is cool and still. It's like shutting the door on the whole city.

Pops took me to the quietest room in the library, the Rose Main Reading Room. He showed me the full set of Encyclopedia Britannica across a long wooden shelf. Twenty-three volumes. Pops patted them all as though they belonged to him.

"Anything you need to know..."

I trace my hand along the spines, looking for the book that has Ele...

Electro-Shock Therapy: The technique passes alternating currents of electricity through the head, between two electrodes placed over the temples. The passage of the currents causes an immediate cessation of consciousness and a convulsive seizure.

The words make me feel like ants are crawling along my arms. Electricity through Pops's brain. I look up seizure.

Seizure: The act of seizing, or state of being seized, sudden and forcible grasp or clutch.

Grabbing his brain. Sudden. No sudden movements.

But maybe his brain has to be taken by surprise to shake everything back in place. To make it better. Ollie sometimes grabs Stan by the scruff of her neck when he wants to wash her.

He always gives her a little shake.

Maybe it isn't so bad.

I close the heavy book and leave the dark of the reading room to stand outside in the late spring air. Linden blossoms whirl and spin down, dotting Patience's rump. I lean against the ledge and reach up to stroke her stone paw.

Being Strong

On the last day of sixth grade, Pops is still not home from the hospital.

Everyone in the classroom is busy getting ready for the end-of-year show. Mrs. Nault knows that Pops is in the hospital. She said I don't have to be in the play. I think she knows I don't want people looking at me.

The air in the classroom is fizzy with excitement. Everyone is putting on costumes. Being nervous.

Mrs. Nault said I can be Lady Murasaki's lady-in-waiting, Lady Saisho. A lady-in-waiting is like a maid. It's my job to turn Corky into Lady Murasaki.

"Hair first."

Even though she isn't on stage, Corky is already pretending that she is more important than anyone else. I drape her shoulders with a painting shirt. I mix a cup of thick black poster paint from Mrs. Nault's supply.

Corky and I haven't talked much since I stayed over. I told her Pops is sick. I didn't say words like shock therapy or seizure. She knows there is more, and I know she's angry because we said no secrets. But my mouth can't work its way around the words.

Today she's too excited about being Lady Murasaki to notice anything about me. I start to spread the paint on her fine blonde hair. As it dries, her hair goes stiff, like the Japanese doll that Mrs. Nault brought to class, the one in the glass case carrying paper pails of water.

I wish I could find a laugh inside me. I'd usually laugh to see Corky with black hair.

"Face next." Corky closes her eyes and holds her face up to me. I think about splattering it with black paint. But I dust white face powder on her, to make it pale. The powder puff sends up small clouds that settle on her shoulders.

"Not too much! Now my mouth." She puckers her lips. I use Gerry's cherry red lipstick to draw her a kiss.

"And now, la pièce de résistance!" Corky hands me the binding cloth. I hold it and she spins happily into my hands. I wrap the kimono around her and tie a large belt at the back. She slips her socked feet into thong sandals.

"How do I look?"

She's a different person. Foreign. Mysterious. Cold. She is a stranger.

I feel a croaking inside me, like the start of

some squawking saxophone solo that hurts your ears. I swallow hard. I do the only thing I can. I bow. Corky returns the bow formally and turns away, dismissing me like a servant.

When it is her turn to go on stage, she walks with tiny, lady-like steps. She fans herself delicately and starts into Lady Murasaki's story.

"The Emperor knew that the time had come when, little as he liked it, he must let her go. But that she should slip away without a word of farewell was more than he could bear..."

The audience is silent. Corky is transformed, painting pictures from words written a thousand year ago.

"...he called her by a hundred pretty names and weeping showered upon her a thousand caresses; but she made no answer..."

Corky puts her hands together and bows reverently to the applause. The lights snap off. The stage is dark. But she stays in place.

In the darkness, she says our favorite line of Lady Murasaki's.

"Real things in the darkness seem no realer than dreams."

That was my idea. To say it after, in the dark. I mouth the words in the wings, in the dark.

Real things in the darkness seem no realer than dreams.

If Pops loses his memories, then maybe the dark nights at the Hickory House and the Vanguard were only dreams after all.

The Shocks Leave an Empty Shell

He is home.

Back from the hospital, he sits. Silent.

For two days, he sits. Still.

For two days, Mom and I tiptoe around the house of the person who is not there.

I leave peanut butter on rye crackers on his desk.

I try to write poems, but there are no words in the silence.

I thought that a fresh start would mean starting over. Picking up the record needle, going back to the beginning. That we'd go to Coney Island. We'd go to Willard's house-inside-the-synagogue. We'd leave each other poems. He'd drum and go to work. Ira would come back.

That Mom could go to the studio again.

That the time signature in our lives would be 3/4.

He sits, and I am afraid of what he has forgotten.

The New Song

On the third morning, there's a song beside my bed. There is no stone or shell. The time signature is 7/13, which isn't a signature at all.

> *There's no chance for you*
> *To digress*
> *On the Broadway express*
> *When I live on 8th Avenue.*
> *Earlobes*
> *Fingertips*
> *Bent toes*
> *We'll hear no more sirens*
> *In nature's environs*
> *Ambivalence*
> *Equivalence*
> *Fragments*
> *Civil Aunts*
> *But the END of the world is SEISMOLOGY*

I look up seismology in the dictionary.
Seismology: The study of earthquakes.
I fold the paper. I put it in the bottom of my dresser drawer under my socks.
I don't put it in my heart-shaped box.

Real Things in the Darkness

His chair is empty.

For an empty day, Mom and I orbit his empty chair.

At night I'm jerked out of sleep by drumming. I am in bed in the dark, and there is drumming.

He is back. But the drumming is a storm unleashed — Thwack-Smash-Zing-Da-Da-Da-Da-Ching-Ching-Ching-Whomp-Zing-Bang-Bang-Bang — and I am blind under my covers. Hearing, not hearing. My pillow over my head.

Banging.

Thelonius Monk on the record player, full volume.

Thwack-Smash-Zing-Da-Da-Da-Da-Ching-Ching-Ching-Whomp-Zing-Bang-Bang-Bang —

Shouting.

Where is Ira? I hold Mr. Carter the bear.

Thwack-Smash-Zing-Da-Da-Da-Da-Ching-Ching-Ching-Whomp-Zing-Bang-Bang-Bang —

Strange voices shouting.

And then quiet.

Quiet that fills my head like screams.

I push away from blankets and pillows and safety.

I'm in my nightgown at the edge of the dark. My feet are bare, still warm from bed.

The living room is a foreign country filled with Pops. Pops in white pants streaked with grimy gray, his puffy vermilion ski jacket torn, the stuffing pouring out like Stan throwing up a fur ball.

Mom a statue, her Christmas dressing gown pulled tight. Staring at two men. Strangers.

Two strangers.

And one gun.

I am a ghost that no one has seen.

Mom's voice quiet. "Please leave. Now."

"Shut up, bitch!" SLAP.

And the room shatters.

And I am under the table.

I don't know how I got under the table.

I know there is a gun.

I feel my strong mother's heart beating through my back, keeping my own beating, not stopping, stopping here, curled under the table, my strong mother's arms holding, holding, holding me tight, making me small, making me invisible.

I don't know how I got under the table.

I know there is a gun.

I know I am awake.

I hear the men not Pops—words—but my

ears are shut down. The words are sounds, not meaning.

I don't know how I got under the table.

I know there is a gun.

The sounds make words like knives.

"We're giving you two days. Two days is what you've got."

There is no breathing under the table.

"You've had the junk. We want the money."

I smell the sharp cat pee smell in the carpet under the table and remember Stan's nest where she had Sailboat, remember her strangled cries as she pushed the tiny kitten out of her body, and later the bloody mass that was the placenta, and I wonder when I last put flowers on his grave.

I don't know how I got under the table.

I know there is a gun.

I know I am awake.

I know there is a gun.

I see Pops's bare feet, wonder at his toenails, perfectly shaped and clean from the hospital where the fresh start was supposed to begin.

I chew and taste blood, the taste of the blood that pumps through my body, the taste of the blood that makes my heartbeat, my strong mother's heartbeat in my back, knowing, and not knowing, that nothing, nothing will ever be the same.

TWO

147 East 17th Street
New York
June, 1963

A Different Fresh Start

The taxi finds streets I have never seen.

We left 5D with two suitcases. Pops was not there.

We couldn't go to 4D. He would find us in 4D. The men would find us in 4D.

We sleep together in the same bed in a small hotel room without Stan, without Ollie. Then there are nights when we sleep on a blur of couches.

We leave no trace. Not even for Ira. We cannot be found. Not even by Gerry and Corky and Patty.

What Mom tells me:

I love Pops very much. But
> *We can't make him well.*
> *We can't help him.*
> *Ira can't help him.*

I love Pops very much. But
> *We have to leave. Just you and me.*
> *We have to be safe.*
> *Stan and Ollie will live with Corky and*
>> *Patty.*
> *Ira will look after Pops, if he can.*

I love Pops very much. But

> *He has to stay away from us.*
> *He has to get clean.*
> *I love Pops very much. But*
> *We have to stay away from him.*
> *We have to be strong.*
> *We have to become invisible.*
> *I love Pops very much. But*
> *He must not know where we are.*

Late summer days, hot summer nights. We become invisible. We see only strangers.

Mom needs time. Time to find a new job. To find us a bed. A new table. She leaves me with friends of friends of friends who have a summer cabin on an island and a daughter who is almost the same age as me.

"I'll be back when I've found us an apartment. When I've found a job. You are safe here."

I do not feel safe.

The girl and her small brother argue and push all day long. I read *Heidi* alone, sitting on rocks, ignoring the water that rolls between my toes.

Days stretch to weeks. Light hurts my eyes. Food hurts my stomach. I scratch the mosquito bites on my legs until they bleed.

Trust your momma . . .

There are no paradiddles on the wall, secret

nights of music, new words or poems by my bed.

Has Mom gone to her studio? Is she making colors dance and forgetting?

Did Pops find the money for the men? Did he remember?

147 East 17th Street

Six wide stone steps.

Cold stale air blots the heat of the sidewalk. A row of metal mailboxes covers the left wall. Envelopes and flyers dot the floor. There's a sour, heavy cooking smell. I feel it seep into my clothes.

Mom unlocks the inside door that leads to the different fresh start.

"We're in number 6. Three floors up."

There's no elevator.

My foot slips on a loose piece of cracked linoleum. A no-color color, a grayed-out color like the newel post I grab. My hand barely fits around the fat banister. It feels like I'm walking through molasses to get to the first landing. Turn. Walk past number 2, number 3. Turn. Next flight up. Turn. Past number 4, number 5. Turn. Next flight up. With each step the air thicker, hotter, filled with unfamiliar smells. Up and turn. First on the right. Number 6.

"I'll get keys made for you."

The door makes a rough scrape as it pushes over more linoleum. It might have been yellow once. Yellow with white flowers. Maybe.

"Always remember to slide in the deadbolt."

A doll's kitchen no larger than the one in Willard's storybook house. Tiny fridge, tiny stove, tiny sink. A drip hits its rust-stain mark.

"We've got our own bathroom." Through the door off the kitchen a tiny tub, tiny toilet, tiny sink. Doll bathroom.

Kitchen and living room all in one. Empty except for a single bed.

"I'll sleep here. You'll have the bedroom."

A door opens to a room filled with a bunk bed.

"I got a good deal on the bunks. I thought Corky could stay over sometimes."

These beds are not my bed. These beds are covered in rough green covers. A thin wood ladder leads to the top bunk. Sitting on the pillow of the top bunk that is not my bed is Mr. Carter. The bear Ira won. For me. At Coney Island.

The window that is not my window looks out at the side of another brownstone.

"We'll get more furniture. Over time. The job is good. Receptionist at a publisher's. And they'll give me manuscripts to type on Saturdays. Extra work, extra money. I can get a typewriter at the pawn shop. Next month."

That night we sit on the floor and eat rice and

chili out of wooden bowls. We have two bowls, two plates, two forks, two knives, two spoons, two cups, three beds, and one stuffed bear.

WHEN BROWN IS GRAY
by Miranda Billie Taylor

*A brownstone is a building made of brown
    stone.*
*Uptown the brownstones are burnt sienna or
    elegant sand.*
But number 147 East 17th Street
is a brownstone that's tombstone gray,
not raw sienna mixed with indigo and lake,
not soft like Payne's gray,
*not grayed-out like complementary colors
    together*
but brown that is gray like rain.

How to Make a New Home

Early Sunday morning. The city August hushed. The salty, wormy smell of the fish market. A row of houses waiting to be torn down.

The sign on the scaffolding says Tepperman.

Mom and I slide noiselessly behind the scaffolding. Doors aren't locked when houses sit quietly waiting for a wrecking ball.

"House Wrecking," she calls our Sunday adventure. An outing to furnish the apartment.

We move through deserted rooms. Other people's memories. A broken chair, stained curtains, chipped plates, papers. Garbage. Mom carries a screwdriver in her purse, ready for prizes. A pretty brass doorknob, a curtain rod.

Mom shows me how to detach a telephone attached to a box on the wall by wires.

"When we get back to the apartment, I'll show you how to reattach it. You have to make sure not to connect the yellow wire. That one would tell the phone company that we're using the phone. If you don't attach it, they won't know. So we can use the phone for free. A trick I learned from my mother."

In the hall, a stained-glass window polishes

the fall sunshine, and the grimy wood floor of this Tepperman house dances with ruby red, forest green, ultramarine. Mom helps me pry the window from the transom—a new word from Mom. It's my prize.

Colors to decorate the dark of my window in Apartment 6, 147 East 17th Street.

P.S. 22

This fresh start means seventh grade in a new school. Best Friends Seminary costs money. P.S. 22 is free.

I wonder if Corky has a new best friend at Best Friends Seminary.

I put on my old beige jumper. I fold dingy ankle socks over scuffed Buster Brown shoes. I put the white heart-shaped stone in my pocket before taking it out and leaving it in my heart-shaped box. I put my keys in my pocket instead.

I pick up the paper bag Mom has left, with the peanut butter sandwich made on Arnold's Bread.

> Out the door,
> lock the deadbolt,
> down the stairs,
> out the glass door,
> out the wood door,
> down the steps
> and up 17th.

> Sirens scream.
> Car horns holler.

Turn right at the corner,
up and away
on Second Avenue,
crossing 18th,
past the spilled trash,
over the dog piles,
around the man with no legs
and no money,
past the drugstore,
laundromat,
O'Malley's Bar,
two blocks up
through the chainlink fence,
through the gravel playground
with the broken swing
and up to the dark glass doors,
to seventh grade
at P.S. 22.

I work to be invisible at school. I count doors, find rooms, melt into my seat.

"Miranda Taylor?"

"Here."

And I am invisible again.

Mom says it's okay to be visible again. She says it's okay to see Corky if I want.

But I don't. Being invisible is safe.

The world of P.S. 22 is a foreign land of jokes and laughter, elbows and anger, teasing and threats. I am silent like the Meeting Room in Friends Seminary. I carry the silence all day, through the bells and alarms, the chatter, shouts and whispers. I take small sips of air, careful not to disturb the currents.

At three-thirty I let the flow carry me out the door.

    Sirens scream.
    Car horns holler.

    Through the playground,
    through the fence,
    past O'Malley's Bar,
    the laundromat,
    the drugstore,
    around the man with no legs
    and no money,
    over the dog piles,
    past the spilled trash,
    around the corner,
    up the steps,
    through the wood door,
    through the glass door,

up the stairs,
turn, walk, turn, up, turn, walk, turn, up
to number 6
where my key fits into the deadbolt
and the silence waits.

Knock-Knock Who's There

A knock at the door.

Tap, Tap-tap-tap-tap. Tap, tap.

Shave-and-a-haircut. Two bits.

That's Corky.

Not Pops.

Pops would ding-ding-da-ding-ding-da-ding.

Corky is always Tap, Tap-tap-tap-tap. Tap, tap.

Corky knows where I am. Does Pops?

All I want to hear is ding-ding-da-ding-ding-da-ding.

Corky is 4D and number 525 East 14th Street.

Corky is not number 6, 147 East 17th Street, where there is no furniture.

17th Street is not far from 14th Street, but number 6 is a lifetime from 5D.

Corky is Friends Seminary School, not P.S. 22.

Tap, Tap-tap-tap-tap. Tap, tap.

I have no space for Corky in number 6, 147 East 17th Street. I have no words for Corky in number 6, 147 East 17th Street.

I have no ears to hear about Gerry and Patty and the pizza man on First, about Friends Seminary, about being in a play, about Mrs. Nault, about French homework. About Stan and

Ollie who live with Corky now.
I listen to her feet clomp down heavy stairs.

Working on Not Thinking

In art class, Mr. Peterson tells us how to draw shadows with thin straight lines.

I use the side of my pencil, shading the way Mrs. Nault showed us.

"Miranda. That's not the way I showed you. Please do it the same way as everyone else." Mr. Peterson hands me a fresh piece of paper. "You'll never make new friends if you start by showing off."

The girl behind me giggles. I don't know her name. I imagine piercing her ivory skin with my pencil, vermilion blood spurting from the wound and speckling her lemon yellow blouse.

I have to learn to stop thinking.

In English class, Miss Yeoman says that all poems must rhyme.

"Modern poets are just too lazy to make their poems rhyme. The poem 'Daffodils,' by William Wordsworth, is the greatest poem ever written. It has both rhythm and rhyme and makes a beautiful picture." Miss Yeoman stands in front of the class, her outstretched hand bouncing with each emphasized syllable.

> "I **wan**dered **lone**ly **as** a **cloud**
> That **floats** on **high** o'er **vales** and **hills**,
> When **all** at **once** I **saw** a **crowd**,
> A **host**, of **gol**den **daffodils**;
> Be**side** the **lake**, be**neath** the **trees**,
> Flu**ttering** and **danc**ing **in** the **breeze**."

She says Fluttering as "Flut'tring."

That would never work in a tanka.

"Now, class, all together . . . I **wan**dered **lone**-ly **as** a **cloud** . . ."

Pops's brushing. Swish-tick-a-swish-tick-a-swish. The sound of the city, waves of cars and taxis. Swish-tick-a-swish-tick-a-swish.

Miss Yeoman's poetry. De-**dum**, de-**dum**, de-**dum**, de-**dum**. Marching in a circle. Marching to a gray nowhere. Marching in black and white.

Strays

Last bell. I leave the yard. I leave the fence. I pass O'Malley's Bar. The laundromat. The drugstore. Turn left.

Leaves fall on open cans. Open cans of cat food.

Cat food under every tree. Someone leaves open cans of cat food under every tree.

Under every tree, cats. Black, tabby, gray. Skinny, scrappy, skittish.

Cats under every tree.

Cats that aren't Stan and Ollie.

But they let me pet them anyway.

Number 6 Is an Island

We do not talk about the table.

I still feel the beat of Mom's heart through my back.

I still don't know how we got under the table.

I know there was a gun. I did not dream the gun.

We do not say words.

Words like gun. Words like Junk. Smack. Heroin.

Words like electroshock therapy. Words like seizure.

The drawbridge at number six is pulled up tight.

We are an island where no one comes in, and no words are said.

It Takes Three Tankas: Number One

Tap, Tap-tap-tap-tap. Tap, tap.
I listen as the silence crackles.
Schloop.
A piece of paper slides under the door. Steps clomp down the stairs.

A TANKA TO FINISH

School is different.
Some things are the same. Like me.
Your best friend, always . . .

I take the paper into my room. My room has a bunk bed, a suitcase of clothes and a stained-glass window.
I pretend a lot of furniture in my room.
A rock for my dresser.
A leaf for my closet.
A pigeon feather for Pops's chair. Mom doesn't know about that one.

I put Corky's tanka under the rock that is my dresser drawer.

There is no place for Corky in my pretend furniture.

Missing Ira

LOST
by Miranda Billie Taylor

Cups of hot milk.
Hugs that smelled like adventure.
Smiles wrapped in safety.
A laugh the size of a millionaire's mansion.
Tears like a sudden thunderstorm on a
*   summer afternoon.*
You were supposed to be there when we
*   needed you.*
When there was a table.
When there was a gun.

New Rhythms

On Saturdays, Mom does not go to the studio because Mom doesn't go to art school anymore.

On Saturdays, Mom and I buy groceries for the week. After toast.

"Never shop on an empty stomach." She tries to make it into a game. "How much change will we have from a twenty-dollar bill? Can we make it more?"

She means can we manage with one less potato?

No.

Do I really need lettuce in my sandwich?

Yes.

Do you like this brand of peanut butter?

It tastes like mud.

They aren't real questions, so I don't answer. I push the cart.

After shopping, Mom starts her weekend typing job. Clack-clack-clack-ding! Clack-clack-clack-ding! She wallops the typewriter carriage, starting each new line like she's punching someone. She types while I make a big pot of chili—no-meat-just-beans-and-tomatoes-and-spice—enough to last most of the week when we eat it with rice.

"Beans and rice go together." She says it every week. "Beans and rice are a complete protein. If you add a bit of cheese."

There is no cheese.

Clack-clack-clack-ding! Clack-clack-clack-ding!

I want her to stop clack-clack-clack-ding.

"Go together like Fred and Ginger?" I ask.

She looks up mid-wallop.

"Yes." A tiny smile. Like I've given her a present. Like Fred and Ginger are a precious gift. "Like Fred and Ginger." And she gets up and starts a new rhythm. Not clack-clack-clack-ding. But a soft shoe. "Step-shuffle-ball-change. Step-shuffle-ball-change."

I see Fred and Ginger guide her to the dance floor and she stretches out her arms.

"Step-shuffle-ball-change. Step-shuffle-ball-change."

I leave the chili cooking, blurp-blurp, and add my feet to slap, "Step-shuffle-ball-change. Step-shuffle-ball-change."

Clack-clack-clack-ding. Blurp-blurp. Step-shuffle-ball-change.

The new rhythms of our lives.

Words Lost Under the Table

Pops made sense of the world through the
    bounce of a drumstick.
Mom made sense of the world through the
    twirl of a brush.
But Mom is not painting and Pops is drum-
    ming in 7/13 time.
    This world doesn't make sense.

Pops said I was a poet.
He taught me to hear the sounds,
    to find the words in the sounds,
    words that jangle and jump,
    the jagged edges of jazz,
    the ping and punch and ricochet of high-
        hat, snare and tom.

But the lines, curves and dots I need are
    lost under the table.

It Takes Three Tankas: Number Two

I turn the flat silver mail-slot key and there's a letter addressed to me. Inside the envelope is a paper with the first three lines of a tanka. It's like a message in a bottle, a message from a foreign land.

A TANKA FOR MISSY AT CHRISTMAS

I miss you a lot
Where are you this Christmas Eve?
You're still my best friend . . .

Inside the envelope there's an envelope with a stamp on it. An envelope addressed to Corky Fisher. #525 East 14th Street, Apartment 4D.

Apartment 4D is the same.

But someone else lives in Apartment 5D. Someone else uses the mailbox for apartment 5D.

I put the unfinished tanka under my rock.

Side by Side

Christmas morning slinks in, full of icy drizzle.

Our miniature Christmas tree sits on the table. Last night we sewed popcorn onto threads and twirled it around the tree for decoration.

Last year there was a proper tree with ornaments and lights and tinsel. Last year we did Family Portrait. Last year the floor was piled with shiny wrapped boxes.

This year there are three presents wrapped in brown shopping-bag paper. One from me to Mom. Two from Mom to me.

All I want is a card from Pops. All I want is a poem.

Mom opens my gift. It's a drawing of Stan and Ollie, with all the right shading, just like Mrs. Nault taught me. I did it from memory. I know she misses them too.

I open Mom's gift. It's a dark green jumper with matching brass buttons on the straps and pockets. I could hear her sewing at night.

"I hope it fits. You're growing so fast. I hope you like it."

I make my face work itself into a smile. "Thanks."

"I have something else. It's pretty special."

She hands me a box the size of our bread box. The brown shopping-bag wrapping paper is decorated with painted colors. Cadmium orange, alizarin red and violet vibrate off the brown paper. But they fall flat at my feet.

I take the box from her.

"You might want to sit on the floor to open it."

I sink down and deliberately tear the paper, the paper she has so carefully painted.

I lift the lid. Inside, tucked into a buttery soft cloth is a camera. Pops's Hasselblad.

My head jerks back.

"His camera is not yours to give away!"

She glares down at me. "Would you rather I sell it? We could sure use the money. There's probably two months' rent in that camera!"

"No! You can't sell it! It isn't yours to give or sell!"

I look down at the camera. He didn't take it. He left me and Mom and his camera. He must be coming back. He wouldn't leave his camera.

I slip my hand down into the box.

The Hasselblad's black bumpy skin warms in my hand. I lift it out carefully and hold it against my chest. I flip the strap over my head, press a button and the viewfinder snaps into place. It seems to come alive.

With the lens cap on I see only my own reflection. An empty space.

I suddenly remember the last Family Portrait. *Smile, Goddamn it.* Is it there? Can I take it out? Develop it? See us together us on a contact sheet?

"There's no film in it." Her voice snaps like a dry twig. Mom the mind reader. "There's nothing there." Did she take it out? Did he?

I push the crank and wind the non-existent film. Breathe in. Hold. Press my finger down. Exhale.

Mom is busy tidying up nothing. The nothing that is, that was, Christmas.

"I'll look after it." I say it to myself, but loud enough for her to hear.

She crumples the painted papers into the trash.

I'll keep it safe until Pops comes back.

The camera's click is a promise. He'll come back.

My Thirteenth Birthday

Chili with beans, no meat.
Butterscotch cake, from a mix.
A card from Corky.
Mom and me.
Side by side.
Thirteen candles.
One wish.

Being Thirteen

Saturday. Mom is busy with clack-clack-clack-clack-ding.

At Eisenberg's diner, near the park, there's a sign. Help Wanted. Saturdays. See Fred.

Fred and Ginger?

I twirl my hair into a chignon bun, just the way Mom does, and carefully draw my lips with Mom's Flame lipstick, the way Ginger Rogers does.

Clack-clack-clack-clack-ding.

At Eisenberg's, Fred the cook runs his thumb along graying stubble. His stained apron strains over a saggy belly. No dance shoes in sight. I push images of Fred and Ginger aside. He doesn't ask how old I am.

"When can you start?"

"Now. Today."

And he hurls me a dingy white apron, his eyes slowly sliding over my non-existent breasts.

I duck my head into the frilly shoulder straps. "What do I have to do?"

"Just give the customers what they want. Hey, Betsy!" He calls over a woman older than Mom. She's chewing a huge wad of gum. "This is Missy. Show her how it's done."

And he's gone and Betsy's working the counter.

"'Nother cup of coffee?"

"Fries with that?"

"Toasted or plain?"

I watch Betsy whirl down the counter, constant movement.

"Hey, miss. Can I get a coffee or what?" Right beside me. Glaring at my frills from under a battered hat.

"Ah, yeah, sure, coming right up."

I copy Betsy's movements, and I'm grabbing cups, pouring, shouting orders to Fred, and giving the customers what they want.

"'Nother cup of coffee?"

"Fries with that?"

"Toasted or plain?"

Each time I smile, I get a tip. At the end of the day, Fred hands me a five.

"See you next week."

My legs ache. All I want is a bath. But in the reflection of the plate-glass window, I'm smiling.

On the way home, I pass a pawn shop. I see a tortoiseshell hairpin in the window. Like one Mom used to have. I ask the man to wrap it for me and he rolls it in some used tissue paper.

"Find your own ribbon," he says, handing me the change.

I'll put the change in our savings jar.

Eisenberg's isn't Al's or the Automat, but maybe it's part of the new fresh start.

My Thirteenth Birthday: Take Two

I open the mailbox with my tiny flat key. There's mail.

> *To Miss Miranda Billie Taylor, herself, 13 years old*
> *147 East 17th Street*
> *#6*
> *New York, New York*
> *On the Earth*

Fat red grease-pencil words.
Pops.
He knows where I am.
Words to the edges of the envelope.
The envelope covered in drawings. Horses, birds, roller coasters.
The number 13 over and over.
And in the corner, covered by a drawing of a cat:

> *Hotel Chelsea*
> *222 W. 23rd St.*
> *New York, New York*

I know where he is.

I carry the envelope like a whisper from the mailbox to my room. I carefully lift the flap. Torn paper falls out like confetti. Torn paper, torn words, torn puzzle.

I set the pieces on the floor. Turning them, placing them, a jigsaw puzzle of secret words. Until a message emerges from the shards.

> *We are such stuff*
> *As dreams are made on; and our little life*
> *Is rounded with a sleep*

Prospero's lines from *The Tempest*.

Finally, Words

Mom's words ring in my head:
> *I love Pops very much. But*
> > *He has to stay away from us.*
> > *He has to get clean.*
>
> *I love Pops very much. But*
> > *We have to stay away from him.*
> > *We have to be strong...*

But Pops's words are clues. Clues to make him well, to bring him home, to make him safe, to make us a family again. A different kind of being strong.

I search *The Tempest* for more clues, for clues to what he wants me to do. And I find one. At the end of the play, Prospero knows his brain has been weakened.

> *Bear with my weakness, my old brain is*
> > *troubled.*
>
> *Be not disturb'd with my infirmity.*
> *If you be pleas'd, retire into my cell,*
> *And there repose.*

I read it slowly, over and over until I understand Pops's clue to me.

It means he is weak. His brain is in trouble. *Be not disturb'd* means not to be afraid. *If you be pleas'd, retire into my cell.* He sent it to me because he wants *me* to find him in his caged cell. *And there repose* means to stay there and be calm. And then he wants me to stay and talk to him.

I turn to the end of the play. It ends in a rhyming couplet.

"A rhyming couplet brings everything home," says Mrs. Nault.

> *As you from crimes would pardon'd be,*
> *Let your indulgence set me free.*

He wants to be forgiven! He needs to know that we forgive him.

If I can see him, I can let him know. I can let him know we love him. That we forgive him. If I can see him, I can bring him back his memories.

He wrote to me. He needs me to help him remember.

Casual Lies

Every day, I say a magic charm. I repeat it thirteen times a day. Thirteen, like me.

> *As you from crimes would pardon'd be,*
> *Let your indulgence set me free.*

I don't tell Mom.

He wrote to me.

Our secret, like the Hickory House, the Vanguard.

My secret. I can help him remember and bring him home and everything will be fine again.

I wait for the right time, a time when Mom won't notice.

Mom calls me every afternoon to make sure I am home. I make dinner every night after school. So I have to wait until a Friday afternoon, when she calls to say, "I have to work late, a drink with the boss after, don't wait up."

"That's fine, Mom. I have a lot of homework. See you in the morning."

And I build a false Missy from my nightie and sweaters, just like Pops showed me. I tuck her in carefully. I can sneak back in while Mom sleeps. Like I used to do with Pops.

I write out the charm on a fresh piece of

paper in my best handwriting.

I put his torn clue into its envelope with the hotel address printed on it.

I put the envelope into my pocket. I put the folded paper into my pocket. Two halves of a code.

I think about taking his camera, but I know it's not a good idea to carry it on the subway. But I'll tell him I've got it. That I'm keeping it safe. For him to build new memories.

Crossing the Night to the Chelsea

It isn't far to West 23rd Street, but I have to go by subway. I have to walk down to 14th Street, to the subway at 3rd that was our station before.

I've never traveled on the subway alone at night. Standing room only. I grab the metal pole in the middle of the car. I spread my feet wide to keep my balance as the train jerks and sways. There are other hands holding the pole. Fat, sticky, warm, wrinkled. I keep moving mine so that we don't touch. If I was taller, I could reach the bar at the top.

There are puddles from melting snow dripping off coats and boots. The stale air is filled with the heavy smell of wet wool.

"Who you pushin', man? Get yo face outta my face!"

Angry voices at the end of the car. I see the hands on the pole stiffen. I work to be invisible.

"I said get outta my face!"

I get off at the next station, Union Square, to transfer. I didn't know there would be so many people on the subway at night. I see a scurrying at the end of the platform. Two rats streak down into the tunnel. Beyond them I see a man peeing onto the tracks.

I'm into the train the minute the doors open. Inside, there's a large woman sitting on a pile of old clothes, drinking from a paper bag. A man with wild hair is playing a battered guitar. It's missing at least one string. He's strumming with a broken pen. The sound is tinny and off-key. There's a girl in a long flowing dress, swaying, her beads clattering. But there's no rhythm to the music. Her long hair sweeps in an arc, hitting my hand on the pole. The train brakes squeal as it turns in the tunnel.

I listen for the clattering beat of the train. Ding-ding-da-ding-ding-da-ding.

> *As you from crimes would pardon'd be,*
> *Let your indulgence set me free.*

When he sees me, he'll remember.

The Chelsea

The Hotel Chelsea at 222 West 23rd Street takes up a whole block. A towering red brick wall faces the street, dotted with black iron balconies.

Somewhere in this huge building, Pops is waiting for me. Waiting to be rescued. Even if he doesn't remember.

I glide under the canopy awning.

"Ooompf." A large, tired-looking man bangs into me. A cloud of whisky puffs out and over me. "Beg pardon, miss." An English accent.

He holds the door open for me, as though I belong here. I try to look like I do.

Inside, the walls are covered in a mishmash of paintings—old-fashioned portraits of rich-looking men, messes of drips, city landscapes, women hanging laundry, nudes sunbathing on rooftops, and over the door an engraving of angels and devils. There is one with sweeping colors that reminds me of Mom's paintings. I suddenly wonder what happened to them.

The Hotel Chelsea lobby looks like it means to be fancy, like the Plaza. Mom and Pops and I went to the Plaza hotel once. I was six years old and I loved the book *Eloise* so of course I wanted to go to where she lived, even though I knew she wasn't a real person. Pops took us all to the Plaza and we sat in the Palm Court where there were chandeliers and sculptures and palm trees everywhere. We had plates of tiny cakes that we chose from a tea trolley and tea in china cups and we held our pinkie fingers in the air when we sipped our tea to show we were rich.

But the Hotel Chelsea lobby looks like it's too tired to care about pinkies in the air. It looks like a room that has shrugged its shoulders. There's a thin bleached-blonde woman asleep on a cracked red leather armchair. She'd be beautiful if her cheeks weren't smeared with mascara, if there wasn't a small bubble of spit floating between her scarlet lips.

You'd never see that in the Plaza.

"Can I help you?"

I turn around. A tiny man in a large bow tie is standing behind a counter. Behind him is a wall of cubby boxes. Each box has a number, some with keys, some with letters.

A deep breath. "I'm looking for my father."

The man waits.

"He's staying here."

There's a loud clatter from the hall. A man in a red uniform folds up a fancy brass door. It's an elevator with glass walls. Someone steps out.

I try to make it be Pops.

But the angry man in the rumpled suit who strides into the lobby is not Pops.

"It's not about Marilyn!" he shouts, smashing keys onto the counter. He storms out the front door.

I turn back to the man at the desk. Make my face strong.

"My father wrote to me. From here." I produce the envelope from Pops.

"What room is he in?"

I look at the envelope. There is no room number. I look at all of the boxes. Hundreds of rooms.

"He needs me to find him."

The bow tie shrugs. "Can't give out personal information. Policy."

I grip the counter. "He *needs* me." My throat aches. The words come out as a whisper.

The man turns away.

Night air fills the lobby as a squat gray woman walks up to the counter and extends an open hand. At the same time, the phone starts ringing. The man at the desk reaches to answer the phone as he gives the woman a key. She moves to the elevator

Without thinking, I step in behind her. The elevator man in the red cap clangs the gate of the door shut.

"Evenin', Miss Wilson." The elevator shudders and slowly rises.

"Evening, Sydney."

I watch through the glass wall as we lift away from the lobby.

The brass dial above the door moves through the second floor, third floor. Up and up the elevator ticks and shudders to the top. P.

P for Penthouse. The elevator man pulls back the brass lever, unlocks the door and folds back the gate. The woman steps out, and I follow her onto the red carpet.

Only when the elevator has headed back down does she turn to face me.

"Who you looking for, honey?"

She has kind eyes. Eyes that might be like a grandmother, if I knew what that looked like.

I try to sound grown-up, not desperate. "My father. He's here, but I don't know which room."

She narrows her eyes, as though she is trying to hear me better. "Lots of people come here to get lost," she says.

"He doesn't want to get lost. He's just forgotten who he is."

"Mmmm." She starts to head down the hall.

"He's a drummer," I call after her.

"Lots of musicians here," she says over her shoulder.

I finger the envelope in my pocket. I follow the gray shape down the hall because I don't know what else to do.

She stops in front of a door.

"George is a musician," she says over her shoulder. She unlocks the door, walks through and leaves it open.

I follow her in.

And the shape of the room vanishes.

There are trees in the room. Trees! Huge, twelve-foot-high trees. Shiny, dark green. Jungle green. Trees.

Trees?

"The musicians play on the rooftop most nights. You can ask George."

The air is moist, earthy, full of growth and rot. Soft spongy soil springs under my feet.

"WaKeek-waKeek-waKeek..."

A mynah bird is calling from one of the trees.

I've stopped breathing.

I must be in the middle of a dream.

We are such stuff
As dreams are made on; and our little life

Is rounded with a sleep.

Is this what Pops meant? Is this hotel a palace of dreams?

"George might know him."

My ears tune to the sound of a piano beyond the jungle. Sweet, fluid, like a charm pulling me into the room.

"George, you've got a guest."

The notes stop abruptly and a tall man ducks into the room, his hair scraping the lower branches of the trees.

A huge python is draped over his shoulders.

I am definitely asleep and dreaming.

The snake slithers down the man's body and glides along the floor where I'm rooted, as still as the trees around me. He is coiling himself around my boots, flicking his tongue.

I start to shake. He catches a drop of melted snow as it falls from my coat, then glides off, winding his way up into a tree.

"Make us a bit of hot milk, George, with a drop of Scotch," says the woman. "What's your name, honey?"

I can't make my tongue move. I can't take my eyes off the snake. His tongue is flicking in and out.

"Let's try again." The woman reaches out,

takes my hand and shakes it gently. "My name is May. The man over there making you hot milk is George. What's your name?"

Words form, slowly, quietly.

"I'm Missy. Miranda. Miranda Billie Taylor."

"Well, Missy Miranda Miranda Billie Taylor, sit by the fire. What's your father's name, honey?"

I'm in a dusty armchair by a crackling fire in the middle of a jungle. A mynah bird is perched on the back of my chair, plucking at my head. George who might know Pops is making me hot milk. I think I am in the Hotel Chelsea. It might or might not be a dream.

I make my mouth work.

"Paul Taylor."

May exhales a noisy breath. She glances at George.

"I might have played with him," says George. "Once or twice. Last fall. Drummer guy. Drums on everything in sight. A monster for finding a beat."

"A monster for finding smack," May says under her breath. "Some people are better lost than found."

My heart catches up with the last five minutes and races from par-a-did-dle to anger, clinking in my chest like ice cubes in Pops's drinks.

"He doesn't want to be lost," I snap. "He wants me to find him. He sent me clues."

George hands me a cup of warm milk. I recognize the wet-leaf smell of Scotch, Pops's drink. I think of Ira making me hot milk with sugar. I know I shouldn't drink this milk with the Scotch in it, but the smell makes me feel close to Pops. I know exactly what it will taste like even before it coats my tongue.

George sits and the mynah swoops to his shoulder. May and George and the bird watch me. They expect me to say something.

"He wrote to me. For my birthday." The anger has melted with the hot milk. My voice sounds tiny. Like a small moth. "He wants me to find him," I repeat. "He's forgotten things."

May and George wait. My eyes catch a movement in the trees. The python slithers higher, flicking his tongue.

"Why have you got a python in your... your..." What do I say? In your jungle? "Why have you got a python in your apartment?"

"He's our friend. Why are you looking for your father?"

I don't blink as a tear curls from my eye, alongside my nose, around my nostril and finally rolls over my lips and onto my tongue. It is fat and salty like the sea.

"He needs to know we forgive him."

The fire cracks in the silence. I take the envelope from Pops out of my pocket.

"He wrote to me."

George's eyes skim the drawings on the envelope.

"I need to give him this." I take out the folded paper. "He needs these words. They will help him remember."

The mynah bird is staring at me. George is looking at the paper in my hand.

"Like breaking a spell?" he asks.

I nod.

George reaches out.

"I'll give it to him. If I see him," he says.

I don't want to give the charm to George. I want to do this myself. But suddenly the hotel is too big, and I am too tired and too small.

I put the paper into the envelope from Pops.

"May I borrow a pen?"

George hands me an elegant fountain pen. I write the magic numbers on the outside of the envelope.

Our new phone number.

I press all the love I can into the envelope.

I hand it to George. The tug of the paper is like steel wool as it slides through my fingers.

May stands up. "Come on, Missy Miranda Miranda Billie Taylor. Time to head home."

She guides me down the elevator and through the nighttime world of the Chelsea. The building crackles, like the moment before a sax solo opens up.

"You get yourself home right away. This isn't a place for you to be hanging around late at night."

On the street are high-heeled women in fur coats, men with wild frizzed hair, horns, sirens, pushing and teasing laughter. I shove my hands deep into my pockets and finger the empty space where the envelope and folded paper used to be. I repeat the charm all the way back on the subway and swirling streets, back to #6, 147 East 17th Street, where my key turns silently in the lock, where my eyes adjust to the pitch dark, where my ears listen for Mom's slow breathing, where I silently slide past her and slip into my bed, replacing my false self.

We are such stuff
As dreams are made on; and our little life
Is rounded with a sleep.

The Voice at the Other End

Every day I click the small flat key into the mailbox slot, turn and lift the metal door.

Every day there is no letter.

Mom's working late again. I'm finishing a plate of Kraft macaroni and cheese when the phone rings. Probably Mom telling me not to wait up.

"I need your mother."

"Pops!"

"Put your mother on."

"She's not here. I got your letter. I tried to see you. They wouldn't tell me where you were."

"Where the hell is she at this hour?"

"She's working late." His anger scares me—you gotta be brave—"I miss you, Pops." There's a big sob in my chest. Neither of us says anything for a minute. "Are you—"

"I need some money." Pops's voice is suddenly softer. *"Have you got any money, sugar?"*

I curl around the softness in his voice. "A little. I've got a job. I'm working as a waitress. I've got fifty dollars saved. For camp. Next summer."

I'm talking to Pops. He's on the phone. He remembers me. I'm telling him about my job.

I want him to stay on the phone.

"Has your mother got any?"

"She's not here."

"That's not what I asked." I recognize the growl in his voice, but I don't know the new rules.

"Has she got any money? Is there money there?"

"We keep forty dollars in the drawer. For emergencies."

"It's an emergency. Bring it. Bring it all. Whatever you have."

"Now?"

"Yes, NOW, dammit!" And then, softer. *"Now, honey. Right now. Room 318."*

Room 318. He's in room 318, Hotel Chelsea. I can go to 222 West 23rd Street and help him. I have ninety dollars. Ninety dollars can make him better. I can do this.

"How soon can you get here?"

Mom said the money is for emergencies. It sounds like an emergency. I look at my watch.

"Three quarters of an hour?"

Pops repeats this to someone in the room.

"Okay," he says. *"Three quarters of an hour. Don't dawdle."*

I can make him better. I can help him remember. I can bring him back. Mom will smile again, and we can move back to 5D with Stan and Ollie. I can go back to Best Friends Seminary and Corky will be my best friend again and I can be an angelheaded hipster.

This is something Miranda can do for Prospero. Our secret.

I make another false Missy, to leave in bed. I write a note for Mom.

Not feeling well. Gone to bed early. See you in the morning.

The Chelsea: Take Two

Late night on West 23rd blares and buzzes.
A skinny man in bright purple-and-black striped
pants is leaning on a parked limousine. A woman with long legs and short shiny skirt is tucked
under his arm. They stare as I walk toward the
awning. I clench my fingers around the money in my pocket. They laugh as I open the
door. Pushing into the lobby feels like pushing
through sticky toffee.

The same bleached blonde woman is sleeping, curled on the floor. I think she might be na-
ked under the blanket.

The man with the bow tie at the front desk
isn't there. I slip past the closed elevator to the
stairs, hugging the cool plaster wall, letting my
fingers glide up the tarnished brass rail.

One flight. Muffled sounds down the hall,
murmurs behind doors.

Two. The quiet thud of my feet is absorbed
by the carpet.

Three. Music, a trumpet crooning "Blue
Moon," one of Billie's songs. I listen for drums,
for Pops. But the trumpet stays solo.

Does every room in the Chelsea have a jungle?

Does Pops have a python and a mynah bird? Will we sit by his fire, him with a Scotch on the rocks, me with a plain hot milk with a little sugar, just the way Ira made it?

Past 310, 312, 314, 316. 318. The end of the hall.

The light is dim. Electric wires sway loose from the ceiling. The carpet is threadbare. Graffiti speckles the wall. Phone numbers and swear words are scrawled into the wallpaper.

As you from crimes would pardon'd be,
Let your indulgence set me free.

I uncurl my fingers and do our special knock. Ding-ding-da-di—

The door opens before I finish.

There is a moment.

A moment when everything is going to be all right.

But that moment rips away. I see Pops as though he's a flat photograph in the doorway. He's not wearing a shirt, his chest glistens with sweat, his usually bright-white jeans are streaked gray. His eyes yellow where they should be white. Rough stubble on his face. Hair plastered in wet curls.

There's a sour smell coming off of him.

My eyes shift focus to the room beyond. There is no jungle. It is bare except for a narrow bed and a wooden chair. A man sits behind him in the chair.

There is a gun in his lap.

Time stretches, and snaps. I look at the floor because I don't know where else to look. Pops's toenails are long, cracked. There are lines of dirt between his toes.

"I knew you'd come."

His voice is familiar. A voice that sounds like love.

I look up at him. I want him to hug me. I want him to tell me everything is all right. I want him to tell me that there is no gun. I want him to remember. Coney Island. The Hickory House. The Plaza...

But his eyes flick and don't settle, can't settle, don't see me.

He's looking at my hands. At our hard-earned, hard-saved ninety dollars.

But release me from my bonds
With the help of your good hands.

Pops nods, as though he's heard me. He nods, and his whole spine follows his head as it jerks forward and back. His hands reach toward mine. I want him to hold my hands. Please, please hold my hands in yours. *With the help of your good hands.*

But he pulls the bills away without a touch of skin.

And the door closes.

The door closes, and there are no words.

The Truth

"WHERE THE HELL HAVE YOU BEEN?!"

The false Missy is strewn across the floor. Mom's voice blasts into an avalanche, and the landscape of my life rushes onto the jagged rocks and I'm falling, spinning, and Mom is all I have left, and all I can do is tell her everything. Every secret I've held inside because they were Pops. But Pops is not Pops. All of it, everything special, *our special secret*, tumbles out. My birthday carriage. The Hickory House. The Vanguard. Nights of new words. Drinks lined up on tables. Trane and Dolphy and Jones. Curtains hiding back rooms. Other false Missys in my bed.

I'm wheezing tears, trying to show her the clues, telling her about his letter, showing her Prospero's epilogue. I need her to understand. I can help. I can bring him back. But there's a man with a gun and Pops isn't safe and I need her and I am scared and I'm too little.

I did everything right and he didn't hold my hands and it didn't work.

My face is caked with salt.

All I want is for Mom to make sense of the world.

But when Mom breathes, she says words I don't want to hear.

"He needed that money for drugs. The drugs are a part of his body. He can't live without them."

Rage streams out of my clenched fingers, my frozen jaw. "You said the shocks would help and that he could take a different drug and get better. YOU SAID HE'D GET BETTER!!"

She's very quiet now. "I said he had to *want* to get better."

"But he does want to. HE DOES! He wants to get better. You don't know. He wrote to ME. He sent ME the clues. *You don't know!*"

Mom is staring at her hands. Then her eyes slice into my face.

"Yes, I do know." Her voice is like the snap of a traffic light to red. She is still. "What I know is that you can't make him better. I can't make him better. Ira can't make him better. He's the only one who can make himself better."

And then her eyes fill and it is Mom who is crying. "Loving him won't bring him back. If you give him money, he'll buy more drugs." She's grabbing her breath in huge gulps. "And one day the drugs will kill him."

You gotta look after your momma.

She's gasping, drowning in tears.

And it is me who is holding her. It is my shirt that holds her tears. I hear her words as vibrations through my spine.

"I need you to be safe. I need us to survive."

I finally understand the words I didn't know.

My namesake. "Billie Holiday couldn't live without her smack." The drugs killed her, leaving only her story behind.

The Palm of My Hand

Mom says that Pops would never hurt me.
    But we have to stay away.
    Mom says that if he calls, we need to hang up.
    Mom says we have to look after each other.

Billie Holiday couldn't live without her smack.
    And there was a gun.

One day there is a tiny package in the mailbox.
Addressed to me, with no return address.
    Inside, a flat black stone. It fits perfectly
into my palm. A smooth, flat black stone. Made
warm by my hand.
    A package with no words.
    I put the flat black stone in my heart-shaped
box.

Long Distance

When the phone rings I want it to be him. But also, I don't.

"Hey, Miss Missy. Your momma home?"

"Ira! Where are you?"

"In Naples. Don't have much time. Just money for a moment."

The crackle of long distance. Naples, California. Where Pops grew up. Where he cut off his eyelashes so his mother would stop saying how beautiful he was.

"Tell your momma he's here. On the coast. I'm trying to get him to the hospital, baby. I'm trying. But he won't go."

"Tell him we need him to get better and come home."

"I'm tryin' baby. I'm tryin' to get him clean. Tryin' to bring him home."

And Ira starts to cry.

"I never lost a round in my life, but I'm losin' this one."

Ira crying is like a wounded puppy. It's the saddest sound I've ever heard.

Ira, who is always there.

Ira and Pops. So far away.

Ira, who needs to come home.
Ira, who is at the other end of a dial tone.
And Pops. Who isn't.

I Don't Remember

I don't remember being hit by the swing when I was a year and a half old. But I remember the story Pops used to tell me. In the story, I couldn't sleep and so Pops took me out to the swings. But it was night and dark and the swing hit me in the face and I fell over. I don't remember crying. But I can imagine my lip split open, and blood spilling on my little-girl dress.

I don't remember being in a yellow taxi, rushing to the hospital, zigzagging through the night traffic. But I tell myself the story to help me get to sleep.

Pops is in the front seat yelling at the driver to hurry. Mom is holding me tight in the back.

Pops is demanding they call the best plastic surgeon — "the best one in New York!" — and get him out of his bed in Long Island. "No daughter of mine is going to have a scar on her lip!"

I don't remember the surgeon arriving at two in the morning. I don't remember sleeping through his four tiny, precise stitches, his assurance that there would be no scar.

I remember the story. I remember Pops telling me the story.

I look at my thirteen-year-old mouth. If I pull my top lip tight in the mirror, I can just make out a thin white line, bordered by four tiny white dots.

Making Choices

I step out of the dim gray of P.S. 22 into the bright spring sunshine and Ira is there. I can't stop my smile.

I wait for Pops to jump out from behind. Surprise!

But my smile doesn't spread to my eyes. I see the sag of Ira's cheeks. Ira alone.

We sit on a bench in the park across the street. Ira reaches into his dusty canvas backpack and pulls out half a stale bun. He tears off a corner and throws it on the walk at our feet. Three pigeons immediately flutter down and begin to fight over it.

"He tossed me, Miss Missy. I saved his life and he tossed me away."

Pull, peck, tear. The pigeons duck and flap. He rips off another piece of bun and throws it and the air is suddenly filled with pigeons. A swirling, bouncing, hopping mess of feathers. Pecking, strutting, ripping. Cooing.

Ira's voice is low, like he's talking to himself, like he's not sure he wants me to hear. "He's living with some jive woman."

"What?!"

"Some nothin' no-name woman."

"Pops is living with someone else?!"

"I tell you, it's ugly. So ugly, even I can't take it. An' I seen a lot of ugly in my life." He kicks softly at the pigeons. They scatter then start pecking at his shoelaces.

Pops? With someone else?

"She loves her smack and he loves his smack and they are lovin' their smack together."

Billie Holiday couldn't live without her smack...Heroin, junk, dope, smack, snow...

Ira's hands slap and grab at nothing. "I ask him, 'Man, what are you doin'? What you doin' with this low-life imitation? Miss Missy's momma's the best woman on God's green earth!' But then he looks at me with those ice eyes, those eyes like knives that could slice up my face, carve it and eat it for lunch. 'That bitch locked me up,' he says. 'I'll *never* forgive her.'"

Traffic sounds and sirens snap off. It's only me and Ira in a soundless vacuum.

My voice sounds like rust. "She was trying to make him better...She said she had to." *It's a chance we have to take...*

"I know that. An' you know that." Ira tears off another piece of bun and tosses it out. A pigeon gulps it before it hits the ground. "But he says,

'She put me in that place. She made that electricity go through my brain. It's like she threw the switch.'"

I explode from the bench screaming. "It was to make him well! Mom told me he'd get better! She told me he'd get better and now he's living with someone else and forgotten me!" Pigeons rise like a cloud. "SHE SAID IT WOULD FIX HIM!"

Ira is up, facing me. "Your momma tried to save him. She did what she thought was right."

"BUT IT DIDN'T WORK!"

"Sometimes, when you're drowning, you have to make a choice."

"A *CHOICE*? WHOSE *CHOICE*? NOT MINE! WHAT ABOUT ME? DO I GET A *CHOICE*?" My fingernails clench into my palms. I'm gulping air. I can't make the air come into my body.

I'm dizzy. I'm suddenly scared. I don't know how to breathe. I can't breathe!

Ira is holding his hands in front of my mouth, close, but not touching. His words are quiet, but his eyes are firm.

"Breathe into my hands. Look at my hands. Put your air into my hands." His voice is sure. "Look at my hands. In and out. In and out."

I do. His palms are big, strong, filled with crisscrossing lines. They could hold the world. I feel my breath come in. I blow it out into his hands. I inhale and exhale and crumple back onto the bench.

We sit together as a lifetime passes.

Pigeons strut and coo.

"Not everyone who is drowning wants to be saved, Miss Missy. Your momma and your Captain Daddy Pops made a choice. They chose to save you. What you do with that choice is yours."

They chose to save me?

There was a slap. There was a gun.

He reaches into his backpack again. "He asked me to bring you this."

He holds out a large shell. The outside a rough bleached white, with bumps like the tines of a crown. The inside an open curl, a smooth pink tongue coiled in on itself. "He said if you listen, you can hear him whenever you need."

I run my thumb across the bumps. The inside is cool, secret, swirling forever into the ocean. I put it to my ear and hear the calm sound of the waves. Only the waves. It is a broken telephone, and he is not at the other end.

He said he would always be there.

And there is nothing I can do.

"Is he ever coming back?"

"Ever is a long time, honey."

The pigeons flutter at our feet, wanting more bread. I look down at Ira's hands. They're empty.

The flock scatters as he stands, but they stay close, pecking at his cuffs, hopeful for stray crumbs. Ira wipes down his pants and a few morsels fall.

"Your momma's makin' us some of her special meat loaf."

Meat loaf. Comfort food, Mom calls it.

"Does Mom know? About Pops?"

Ira nods. "She's hurtin'. She's hurtin' bad. But she's more worried about you."

Ira's face has new lines on it. A big fold between his eyes. I tell him what he needs to know.

"It's okay. I'm okay." And I suddenly know that's true.

I kick away the birds as we head across 17th Street. I blink, and each step shows me a different photograph. My eyes are a lens looking out to the world, the world where I live. A future starts to shape itself. A future with a different story.

A story without a character named Captain Daddy Pops.

It Takes Three Tankas: Number Three

Tap, Tap-tap-tap-tap. Tap, tap.
    Not ding-ding-da-ding-ding.
    Safe.
    Schloop.

A TANKA FOR FRIENDS

    I know you're in there.
    Without you, my world is blue.
    Come out. Have a slice…

I make a choice.

    I don't know who I am, but
    I know I still love pizza.

And slide the paper back under the door, outside to the hall. The silence wavers.
    I turn the deadbolt, and a door opens.

Pizza Slice of the Mind

ON NOT GOING HOME
by Miranda Billie Taylor

When we both bite
         a slice
                 at the same time
the cheese stretches between us
         We have to smile to chew it.

On the way to Apartment 4D
         we both
                 pick dandelions
         and put them on Sailboat's grave.

In Apartment 4D
         Stan and Ollie
                 remember me
and purr. I purr too.

I try not to think about
Apartment 5D
upstairs
that someone else calls home.

Each Day Is Part of Tomorrow

Fred the cook likes Corky's white-blond hair and big-toothed smile. Corky gets a job at the diner so we can work side by side. We share bobby pins to put our hair back in tidy buns.

On Saturdays, we walk to work together and afterwards we walk home to 4D where we put our tips in a special jar labeled *Corky and Missy's Travel Fund.*

On Sundays, Mom and I teach Corky about House Wrecking and together we slide past scaffolding. Then we come home with our treasures and sit on the floor of Apartment 6 and play poker. Mom teaches us how. We use matchsticks for betting. You don't need a table and chairs to play 5-card stud.

On Mondays, I help Mrs. Wendell, who lives upstairs. I open cans of cat food for her, because her hands are too stiff. Then we take the open cans outside and put them under the trees for the strays. We talk to the cats until I go home to make dinner. I like making franks and beans on toast.

On Tuesdays, after school, I go to the library. I walk up the library steps past Patience the lion. I sit in the deep quiet of the Rose Main Reading

Room with the fat Webster's Dictionary, searching for new words before I go home to make dinner. I like making spaghetti with tomato sauce.

On Wednesdays, after school, Corky and I go to the museum to learn about Japan and Egypt and Rome and anything else we want before I go home to make dinner. I like making fish fingers and mashed potatoes.

On Thursdays, I go to Corky's after school and visit with Stan and Ollie. Apartment 6 is too small for two cats, and they would never like to be apart. But they sleep with me when I stay at 4D. I stay the night so that Mom can go to her nighttime job at the Coffee Mill. She serves all-day breakfast to famous musicians, artists and actors. She sometimes brings home autographs of people I don't know.

On Fridays, Mom and I go for a slice from the pizza man on First Avenue and we walk in the Village and pretend we are rich. We look through open windows and see full bookshelves and art on the walls. We walk to Gramercy Park and peer through the black iron gates and imagine we are rich enough to have a key to get in. We find Tepperman houses to house-wreck on Sundays.

We repeat this story, until we know it by heart.

Best Friends

At Friends Seminary, Corky is in a play called *The Pirates of Penzance*.

"I get to be a girl pirate named Ruth. Mrs. Nault said you could come and help me backstage, just like before."

But I don't want to go Friends Seminary.

I need to get ready for my end-of-year show at P.S. 22. Miss Yeoman is in charge. Everyone in my class has to prepare a poem to recite.

Marjorie has memorized the daffodils poem. She says Flutt'ring, just like Miss Yeoman does.

Dirk is reciting a poem he wrote about his dog.

Four best-friend girls are lip syncing a song, pretending they are at a wedding. They say that's poetry, too.

I asked Miss Yeoman if I can go last. I want to do something from *The Tempest*, but I don't know which part yet. Miss Yeoman says it doesn't matter. But I know it does.

When school's over, Corky and I are going to spend the summer working at the diner. We're saving money to travel, but we're not sure where we want to go. We've started reading a new book—*Travels with Charley*—so maybe we'll get some ideas. At the end of the summer we're going to a YMCA day camp. Corky's taking an acting class. I'm going take a photography class.

Next year, I'll be going to eighth grade at P.S. 22, and Corky will be in eighth grade at Friends Seminary. But we'll still be Best Friends.

As You from Crimes Would Pardon'd Be

I stand in the wings and straighten my hairband, a hairband Corky made for me out of extra fabric from her Lady Murasaki kimono. Swirls of cadmium orange and scarlet hold back my hair. I wait for my cue — *"Flutt'ring and dancing in the breeze"* — and finger Ira's turquoise ring on its chain around my neck. He's in the audience with Mom and Corky.

In *The Tempest*, Prospero and Miranda live on an island with only spirits, music and poetry for company. Prospero uses his magic powers to make the world the way he wants it to be. But when Miranda grows up, she needs to leave the island. She needs to be a part of the real world.

The only way they can leave and start a new life is if Prospero gives up all of his powers. He draws a circle on the ground, puts his magic in the middle and breaks it apart.

The audience applauds Marjorie and the daffodils and I walk out of the dark shadows into the spotlight. My new dress catches the movement of air. Mom and I sewed it. Together, we picked out the perfect shade of cerulean blue, the shade of Pops's eyes. The shade of the ocean on a sun-drenched day, Mom said.

I cross to stand in the center of the stage carrying a heart-shaped box and wearing a camera around my neck.

I place the box on the stage. I take out
a white stone shaped like a heart
a broken white shell
a gray pebble
a flat black stone
and a large ocean shell with bumps like the tines of a crown.

I set them in a circle. I lift the camera from my neck and place the lens so that it looks out on the world.

I step into the middle of the circle.

I begin the end. Prospero's lines to his audience:

"Now my charms are all o'erthrown,
And what strength I have's mine own,
Which is most faint..."

Prospero's island is an illusion. An illusion made with poetry and magic. He needs the help of the audience to be able to leave, to get back to reality.

"...But release me from my bands
With the help of your good hands..."

He cannot come back until he is ready to give up illusion. Until he is ready to ask for forgiveness.

"As you from crimes would pardon'd be,
Let your indulgence set me free."

I close my eyes and listen to the gentle thud of my heartbeat in my ears. I feel my breath spread down my spine. I exhale and let it go.

When the applause comes, it's a wave washing the shore clean.

I pick up

the white stone shaped like a heart

the broken white shell

the gray pebble

the flat black stone

and the large ocean shell with bumps like the tines of a crown.

I put them in my heart-shaped box.

I lift the camera, with the lens that sees the world, and place it around my neck.

And I walk off stage.

Acknowledgments

These Are Not the Words is a semi-autobiographical novel. There are real people in imaginary situations and imaginary people in real situations. I am not Missy in age or temperament, but she and I share some biography.

Thank you to Karen Li, designer Michael Solomon, and the team at Groundwood Books for believing in the novel and helping to convey the story onto the page. Being published by Groundwood is an honor.

I can't express how deeply grateful I am for the insight, tenaciousness, good humor and friendship of my editor Shelley Tanaka. Shelley made me go where the story needed to go, which wasn't easy. But her refusal to compromise made this the book I wanted it to be. Working with Shelley has been a dream come true.

This novel had its genesis at Vermont College of Fine Arts under the mentorship of Kathi Appelt, Mary Quattlebaum, Louise Hawes and Martine Leavitt. Without their wisdom and guidance, the story would have remained murmuring in dark shadowy corners. I'm especially grateful to Kathi Appelt for her additional support and notes in the years after my time at VCFA.

Details about the Hotel Chelsea were sourced from *Inside the Dream Palace: The Life and Times of New York's Legendary Chelsea Hotel* by Sherill Tippins, as well as from family friend Lloyd Scott.

Drummer extraordinaire Jeff Asselin helped me to hear drumbeats and get them down on the page. Judith Fox Lee helped take me to the Coney Island of 1963 in my mind. Billie James helped with additional family memories. David Hersh and Emmanuelle Zeesman confirmed particulars of Patience, the Library Lion. Ira Carter was a true guardian angel and an inspiration to find the right words. I only wish he was here to see how it all unfolded.

My mother, Laurie Lewis, has always said, "I gave you great copy, honey. Use it." I've taken her at her word and freely availed myself of her memories to create this particular weaving of fact and fiction. Her creative memoir *Love and All That Jazz* provided insights that were unavailable to my child memory. There is not enough gratitude in the world. Thank you for the choices you made.

Tim Wynne-Jones makes everything in my life possible. You were, and always will be, the right choice.

The author with her mother and trumpeter Miles Davis at a rooftop party in Manhattan, 1956.

AMANDA WEST LEWIS is a writer, theater director and calligrapher. She is the author of eight books for young readers, including *The Pact* and *September 17: A Novel.* Her books have been nominated for the Silver Birch Award, the Red Cedar Award, the Children's Literature Roundtables of Canada Information Book Award and the Violet Downey IODE Award, as well as being selected for the White Ravens collection. She has a BFA in Theatre Performance from York University and an MFA in Writing for Children and Young Adults from Vermont College of Fine Arts.

Amanda was born in New York City, where she learned how to hail a cab at age four. She lived on the East 14th Street loop in Stuyvesant Town and went to Friends Seminary with her best friend, Corky. Her father took her to Birdland for her fourth birthday to see Miles Davis, but she was very sleepy and doesn't remember the set. She lives with her husband, writer Tim Wynne-Jones, near Perth, Ontario, and if you look at her lip very closely, you can just see a thin white line bordered by four tiny white dots.